MW01680218

Forgotten VOWS

TORN LOYALTIES

BOOK ONE

GAYLA J. REEL

BRANDI REED

XOXO,
Gayla J. Reel

Publisher: Gayla J. Reel

Editor: Stellar Media

Exterior Design: Graphics by Stacy

Forgotten VOWS

TORN LOYALTIES

BOOK ONE

GAYLA J. REEL

BRANDI REED

To everyone that ever doubted this was possible. I hope your dinner is lukewarm, your socks get wet, both sides of your pillow are hot, and all of your remotes disappear.

&

To my dearest husband…

🖕

I did it.

Dear Reader,

Mental health is important. Forgotten Vows contains content which may trouble some readers, including mentions and depictions of SA.

Chapter One

The fluorescent lights, obnoxiously loud sirens. The stench of disease. Benjamin hated hospitals. They reminded him of loss… and regret. He clenched his chiseled jaw as he stared at the red emergency lights towering over him. Another fucking curveball. Just when he had finally let Chelsea Sanders go.

Less than twenty-four hours ago, he was in Los Angeles. Eyes on the future, and in the middle of a meeting when his assistant poked her head into the room. He tried to dismiss her, but Melanie insisted. "It's about your wife?"

He didn't have a wife. Not anymore.

It was probably another billing issue. That's what he told himself as he walked down the long hall to his office. It happened once before. Chelsea forgot to take his name off her secondary contacts. That's it. She was fine.

A million worst case scenarios ticked through his mind, one after the other. By the time he reached his desk, he didn't even remember Melanie was there.

"I switched them over to Line Two," she said swiftly.

By some miracle, he kept his voice from cracking throughout the entire conversation with her doctor. As forthcoming as the man was about Chelsea's details, he struggled to get any answers of his own.

It wasn't until he hung up that his hands began to tremble. Ben pulled at his tie, flicking open the button on his collar as his chest expanded with deep lungful's of stale air.

Chelsea was in a car accident. She was hurt, alone, and somewhere in the middle of… Texas?

The doctor explained that Chelsea was medically sedated, but was hesitant to give him a prognosis over the phone. What Ben coaxed out of him was bleak, and in that moment the world felt as if it were swallowing him whole.

He didn't even bother with the office. He booked a flight, rental car, then grabbed his briefcase and walked out the door.

Ben navigated the unknown hallways. Once he reached the floor Chelsea was supposed to be on, he checked in with the woman at the front desk and was told to wait for a nurse to come find him. Being inside of a hospital was something he disliked, but it never bothered him the way it did Chelsea. This was one of her biggest fears. His full lips pressed together into a thin line. Nothing good was going to come from this.

Thankfully, it wasn't too long before two competent-looking nurses came to find him and began diving into what was going on with his former wife. His brow furrowed in concern as they recounted the car wreck she was in.

"*Your wife is very lucky to be alive…*"

Ben listened quietly while they went through her long list of injuries and the steps that were already being taken, including Chelsea's sedation, and what the next steps would likely be. The procedure was successful. The pressure in her brain was decreasing. But more than once, they warned, she had quite a laborious road ahead of her. It was odd that in their next breaths, they repeatedly tried to reassure him that her physical recovery seemed promising.

It wasn't his best plan, but he was going to keep his mouth shut about the small fact that they were no longer married. At least until he could gather all the information or until Chelsea spotted him and let everyone know he most definitely was not her husband. They weren't even on speaking terms and hadn't been since the divorce. Chelsea was not going to be happy when she spotted him. Even less once she realized that she forgot to remove him as her only emergency contact. He was the detailed one in their failed marriage, not her.

Chelsea cried out when another bolt of searing pain shot through her head. Where was she? With wild eyes, she looked around the brightly lit room. Everything hurt and bruises discolored every inch of her skin.

What the hell? A hospital?

She needed to find help, and fast. Someone needed to explain what in the hell was happening to her. She fumbled around until she found the call button, then clutched her pale hands to her chest as a loud voice instructed her to wait for someone to arrive.

"Mrs. Black," the nurse entering the room greeted her. She looked nearly as shocked as Chelsea but had enough decency to recover quickly. "You're finally awake, I see." The nurse smiled before coming closer and checking her vitals.

Chelsea sat utterly horrified as she listened to the details of the accident that led to her waking up here, in this bed, in this old-lady nightgown. She stayed silent as a doctor came in and explained her injuries further, what treatments she already went through, and what was still ahead. That wasn't his most shocking revelation, though. No, that came with the realization that it wasn't just the past week or the accident itself that she was missing. Apparently, several years were wiped clean from her memory.

Tears rolled shamelessly down her sunken cheeks as she frantically tried to remember something, anything. But all she could come up with was more questions.

According to her doctor, the most recent memory she could pull to the surface was somewhere around seven, maybe eight, years prior. When she just started college. She was supposed to be taking on the world, not turn into some fragile twenty-something who couldn't even remember what she got her degree in.

So far, the only good news was that every medical professional that examined her was coming to the same conclusion. There was a good chance this would be a temporary bump in the road, that some memory loss was normal with these types of injuries.

"We will run some tests on you soon to get a better understanding of where we are."

She barely heard him. It didn't matter. He was out of answers.

"Mrs. Black?"

Why do you keep calling me that?" And that was how she learned Chelsea Sanders was now Chelsea Black.

Chelsea spent the majority of her day being passed from one nurse to another as they ran never-ending rounds of tests. She was aware that everyone had a job to do, but she was ready to fall out by the time she was finally wheeled back to her room.

The idea that she had a husband whom she couldn't even remember and who was planning to show up at any given time wasn't calming her nerves, either. How was she supposed to be a wife when she didn't even know who she was?

It didn't feel like she slept for long, but a glance back out the window told her it must have been a few hours because the sun was slipping below the horizon. She groaned as she tried to move, but stilled when she heard a voice behind her. "Are you okay?"

She groaned again as she shifted back to see her visitor. "Yeah, I'm," she trailed off as she finally got a glimpse of the man speaking. His voice was almost familiar, and yet she was positive she had never heard it before.

"Chelsea?"

She and this stranger turned their heads toward the door as the nurse stepped into the room and turned on a light. "Chelsea," the nurse softly repeated as she glanced at the man sitting behind her. "Have you two spoken yet?"

Chelsea stared at the stranger for what felt like too long, but then she slowly shook her head. "No. I just woke up."

"Do you recognize him?"

She shook her head. "Should I?"

The nurse frowned. "Well, that's okay, dear," she said, reaching a hand out to pat her arm. "Like we've said, it'll take time." She once again looked past Chelsea to the man now standing next to the narrow bed. Chelsea didn't need to ask. She didn't recognize him, but she knew. She could feel it.

"This is Benjamin Black. Your husband."

Chelsea was sure she must have looked pretty comical in that moment and the next several to follow. Her eyes went wide as she stared in disbelief. She hardly even heard anything else the nurse said before she was gone, leaving her alone with her supposed "husband."

Chelsea swallowed hard as the man everyone claimed to be her husband turned back around. His brown eyes were dark and haunting, and his stare made her feel vulnerable in ways she couldn't comprehend. He had a strong facial structure with beautiful cheekbones, a sculpted jawline that was covered in light stubble. And on top of his gorgeous head were luscious locks of dark brown hair, styled in a way that looked both sexy and professional.

"You're my husband?"

Benjamin sighed, templed his fingers against one another, and looked back at the door out to the hallway before he answered.

"Ex-husband, actually."

Chelsea blinked again. "E-ex-husband?"

"Yes." His voice remained soft and his tone even as he spoke. "You and I got divorced last year."

"Oh." Great. Not only was she married, now she was divorced, too. One of her hands came up to her forehead to rub the building tension. "I'm sorry. This is all just very confusing."

He nodded his head, leaning back some in the chair. "I would imagine so."

"Are we on good terms?" she asked after a few moments passed, unsure of what exactly she was supposed to say to him.

He gave a tight smile revealing white teeth. "No. I wouldn't say that. I was still listed as your husband and emergency contact. That's the only reason they called me. You and I actually haven't spoken to one another in months."

"Oh," she repeated. "They failed to mention the 'divorced' part when you were being brought up."

Another tight smile. "I may have forgotten to tell them." He sighed. "I didn't think they would be up front updating me on how you were doing if I corrected them on that little detail. I was worried about you," he added with a shrug of his broad shoulders.

Worried about her? No one had worried about her since her mother died.

"I'm sure you are on some sort of information overload with everything you've been through. It's a lot to take in," he said. "I really would like to help in any way that I can, Chels. I'm sure you have a thousand questions rolling around and maybe I can provide some insight."

"The questions I have don't even make sense."

"Well, what are some of the last things you remember?"

Chelsea sighed, letting her head fall back against the flat pillow, and began trying to recite some of the latest things her mind could conjure. "I think it was Halloween. Me and Danny were at a costume party on campus."

"That sounds like a little less than a year before you and I met, if my memory serves. I guess there is a lot to catch you up on."

The past week had been absolute hell as far as Benjamin was concerned. He would have easily preferred Chelsea's pretty green eyes to have opened in a blaze of fury, for her to have just popped up and cursed him out like he expected. Like she had been doing every time she saw him this past year. Chelsea's words were sharp as knives. They ripped him to shreds, but he was used to the verbal assault.

But having her not wake up and just lie there in that bed day after day was more than his heart could stand. The silence was deafening. The endless worry of whether she would ever wake up had weighed him down. He spent more time in the last week berating himself for the wrongs that destroyed their marriage than he ever had before. If they never tossed it all away, this wouldn't have happened.

He nearly had a heart attack when the call came in, informing him Chelsea had, in fact, finally woken up. As happy as he was at the news that she was awake, it tore him all the same. He knew what was in store for him next. After everything he had already been through since arriving here, he wasn't sure if he could handle it.

It wasn't until he arrived at the hospital that he was told about her memory loss. He nearly laughed at the horror of it. Fate sure could be cruel. Right when you think you're getting close to hitting the bottom, the dark pit you were seeing gives way to a whole new level below.

Once they were finally face to face, he searched for any sign that Chelsea remembered him, but there were none. There was no anger or hurt in her eyes when she looked at him. No hateful words being flung his way. No accusations. No hint of her knowing anything about their life together. He was a virtual stranger, as far as he could tell. Which made this position he was in even more precarious. He knew that woman better than he knew himself. Could list her ticks quicker than he could recite his childhood phone number. He knew how to make her laugh, cry, and everything in between. There was no way out of this. They were going to break each other's hearts all over again.

Chapter Two

Benjamin sighed when Chelsea asked how the two of them met. That stutter that only surfaced when she was scared was still present. He wished he knew of a way to reassure her that everything would eventually be okay. He was sure she had an endless string of questions not only about him, but her entire life. Chelsea didn't seem to know where to begin. He asked if she would rather call Danielle or someone else, but her sad smile and the way she said "please" struck right in his core.

"I feel like I need to know something," she said. "Anything about myself and those lost years?"

Ben moved around in the uncomfortable bedside chair before clearing his throat. "I was living in New York at the time. I was working at one of the sales offices for Waterstone when I got offered a promotion. The new position required a move to Los Angeles since it was going to be at their corporate office."

"Waterstone?" Chelsea asked, looking like she was trying to place the name. "The hotel chain?"

Ben nodded. "I was just added to their global marketing operations team," he explained. "I was still getting settled in when I got roped into going with a few of my associates to speak to some business students at local colleges. One of those was the University of Saltridge."

"Your friend was in the class we came to speak to," he said after a pause. "You popped your head in to see her, but wound up staying for the entire lecture."

Out of the corner of his eye, Ben spotted Chelsea blushing. It reminded him a lot of the very day he was describing to her.

"While Miss Jennings got a lot of attention with her bold attitude and strange questions, you caught my eye all on your own within the first few minutes," he admitted. "I ended up making a fool of myself when it was my turn to have the floor, using that to my advantage to flirt with you. You were embarrassed at first, but soon enough you were matching me tit-for-tat every step along the way. But then when the time was finally up, you got all shy on me again and made a mad dash toward the door."

"Oh, God." She groaned, which almost made him smile.

"It was all in good fun," he promised. "And I was going to leave it there. You walked out the door and I gathered my things, preparing to head back to Los Angeles. But as I started walking through those halls again, I couldn't get you out of my mind. There were several flyers to a frat party later that evening, so I gave it a shot and went to see if you would show up. I wasn't there long when I spotted you come in. I didn't stand a chance. After introducing me to your friends, you joined me when I asked if you wanted to get out of there. We spent the entire night walking around Saltridge, just talking. About everything, really. The sun was thinking about waking up by the time we finally got you back to your dorm room. I headed back to LA but from that point on, I would come back to Saltridge to see you every chance I got."

"We fell in love?" Chelsea's small voice asked, bringing him back to the present as he got swept up in the memories of the past.

Ben shifted again in the chair. "We did," he confirmed. "Very quickly and very passionately," he added. "We were in love. Stupidly, head over heels, over the moon and back in love with one another. We wanted to spend the rest of our lives together, and neither one of us wanted to waste any time in making sure that happened. You had your reservations about marriage and I sure as hell never intended to settle down before you came along, but all of that went right out the window. And we made it happen. We planned and had a beautiful wedding. We had never been happier, and you never looked more beautiful than you did that day because of it," he told her, his voice softening just the slightest.

Chelsea smiled at that. "It sounds like it was beautiful."

Ben cleared his throat. "It was. It was everything we hoped it would be. And it was the perfect start to our marriage," he told her. "We stayed in Saltridge so you could continue your classes. I continued to work for Waterstone."

"Um, I mean, do we have any children?"

"No," he answered, suddenly sounding drained. "That was something we didn't see eye-to-eye on. I was hesitant, but I eventually came around. We tried for a short time." Ben's thumb slid over to touch the wedding ring that remained on his finger. He gently rubbed the smooth metal, just as he had since the day she put it on. "But sadly, that someday never came to be for us."

Chelsea slowly turned to look at him, and he swallowed hard at the sight. It was a lot easier to keep his emotions under wraps when she was unconscious. Her emerald eyes were swollen and red as she quietly asked him what changed.

Ben had never been happier for an interruption than when the door opened, and a nurse strode in to check Chelsea's vitals and wheel her away to another floor for some more testing. He knew Chelsea meant no harm with her line of questions. He couldn't imagine how difficult all of this was for her. If he was in her position, he would be just as curious, but strolling down memory lane wasn't fucking easy.

Ben practically jumped to his feet when the nurse announced her plans. He wished Chelsea luck before excusing himself from the room, promising to be back to check on her later. He walked to the closest door that would lead him outside and hungrily breathed in the fresh air.

This had been one hell of a day.

By the time Ben returned to the hospital, visiting hours had come and gone. When he reached the double doors, he picked up the phone to get in touch with the nurse's station. After a brief talk with the woman on the other end, the door unlocked.

Ben made his way down the hallway and then stopped at the desk, his best smile in place. "Thank you," he said sincerely to the older woman sitting there.

"Now, Mr. Black," Olivia, the nurse on duty said.

"I know, I know," Ben said, holding his hands out after setting the white carry-out boxes he'd brought with him down. "But my wife just woke up, and I already missed most of the day with her. I know you can't let me back there to see her, but please just bring her some real food for me. I brought a few extra cupcakes just for you lovely nurses."

The woman sighed, then reached down and picked up the phone in front of her. She gave him one hell of a look, though.

"The doctor gave an okay about bringing her the food," she said first, making him give her another smile. "And he said, given the circumstances of her situation, he will even allow you to come in tonight. But only for an hour, Mr. Black. Or until Chelsea gets tired."

Wonderful. The one time he was counting on the damn visiting hours. He was hoping to put off the rest of their conversation until tomorrow. After all, that was the main reason he was so late getting back.

"You'll have to go back out to security and get a tag," Olivia said. "But then you come back this way, alright?"

Chelsea was already eating by the time he made it back to her room. A hint of a smile graced her lips when she looked up at him. "Hello, again," she said.

He nodded as his way of greeting. "I hope you enjoy the food. I figured you might get hungry, and we all know hospital food isn't at the top of anyone's list."

Chelsea nodded her head this time, twirling her fork around to grab her next bite of spaghetti. "Yes, very much so. Thank you."

"There's actually a cafe area here at the hospital that's not terrible," he said. "They have a few restaurant pods set up, a pizza place and deli."

"That doesn't sound so bad. Might have to get my meals from there while I'm still here," she said, then got a new look in her eyes. "Do you know why I'm here?" she asked. "I mean, not the hospital, of course, but what I'm doing in Texas?"

"No, not really. Like I said, you and I haven't spoken in several months. I really haven't known what you've been up to. Before that, I will admit I was keeping an eye on you after we split, but that wasn't healthy for either of us. You were still in California the last I knew," he told her. "I did get in touch with your property manager and explained what was going on with you a few days after the accident. She told me where she thought you were working and put me in touch with them, but that's about it. I paid your rent, what bills I knew of, but I don't know what else might be out there."

"You didn't have to do that."

"I know."

"Thank you."

Ben shrugged, then unbuttoned his jacket before resting against the chair. "I called Danielle. She said she would call Nate, Gregory, and the others. I think she's going to fly out tomorrow, but if not, she will be here the day after at the latest, I'm sure."

Chelsea smiled. "Yeah, she called earlier. We didn't get to talk long, but it was nice to hear a familiar voice, you know?"

"I'm sure that was a comfort, given your circumstances."

A few more minutes passed. Ben looked up at the clock while Chelsea ate. For a second, he thought that she might have forgotten about where they left off, but she prodded her way into finishing their talk from before.

He couldn't help but let out a heavy sigh. "Things were perfect between us for a couple of years," he said. "We argued, though not very often. We had differences in opinion, ups and downs as any couple does. But things were good. Then, it just went to hell. Everything. We both share the blame, though I bear more of that weight than you, to be honest."

"What happened?"

"I got another promotion at the office. I became the senior manager of my department. There were some inside issues going on with the company and there were a few months that really took it out of me. The hours got longer, and the workload taller. You just graduated and obtained your teaching certifications. You wanted your own career, and it was a dangerous mixture. Our hours never seemed to line up, and it felt like we hardly saw each other. Then when we did, it was a toss-up to how it would go. But that's just the tip of the iceberg."

Ben tried not to look at her. He already knew what she was thinking. "An old acquaintance or something showed up, which was a bigger issue that came between us. Any interaction with her was all about business as far as I was concerned, but Veronica came with her own agenda. I did not know this at first, but later it became painfully obvious."

Ben reached his hand up and rubbed his tired eyes. He couldn't remember the last time he got a solid night's sleep, even before this trip to Texas. "You suspected something was off with her long before I ever saw it coming, and you didn't much care for me brushing it off. And by the time I got the full extent of everything, it was too late. Veronica got you to believe a mountain of lies and there was no part of you that wanted to listen to a word I had to say. It didn't seem to matter what I did or what I said. I couldn't show you enough proof that nothing happened. Your mind was made up. I can't entirely blame you, as the encore performance to it all was a damn good trap, but it was all some twisted game. After that, it was just a matter of a couple of weeks before it was more or less over between the two of us. A lot of angry words were said. A lot of tears shed. Yelling. Screaming. Begging. Fighting. When you told me to leave, I did. I was tired of fighting with you. I was tired of being accused of things that I didn't do. So, I just grabbed enough of my things to fit into my gym bag and walked out the door."

Silently, he added how that was one of the worst mistakes he ever made. While leaving that night wasn't a bad idea, using it as the turning point to give up on them was.

When Chelsea first questioned him about the extent of his relationship with the other blonde, her jealousy was amusing, but shit soon hit the fan and it wasn't something to push off to the side anymore. Chelsea may not recall it all, but he sure could.

The business trip where Veronica sprung her trap still made him shake with fury. That weekend cost him everything. He still wasn't sure how Veronica pulled the whole thing off.

Somehow, Veronica got into his room while he was in the shower, preparing for Chelsea's arrival. The next thing he knew, there was a commotion going on in his room. He poked his head out and there Chelsea was, Veronica, too. Veronica, who was not just in his room but with wet hair, wrapped up in a white robe, eating from the platter room service delivered not too long before.

"You stayed in Saltridge," Ben said, bringing himself back to the present. "I stayed in LA so that I would be closer to the office. We pretty much left each other alone for a while. Eventually, you went ahead and filed for divorce. I didn't fight you on it. Just let it be. I hoped maybe some time apart would help, I guess, or calm things down. But it wasn't long before I caught wind that you were in a relationship with one of your old flames from college."

"You made your reasons for doing so very clear, using it to hurt me for what you assumed I had done. The two of us blew up at one another once more, this time far worse. We both lost our tempers grandly that night, saying things we didn't mean, and when Monday rolled around, I went and hired a lawyer. It was all pretty straight-forward. I wanted it done, so I agreed to just about anything you wanted, did my best to keep a cooler head, and ignored the rage fuming from your end.

"That, of course, only made you angrier in the end, but I didn't feel like going back into my turmoil, so I gave up. Before long, our divorce was finalized, and we were no longer husband and wife. We did our best to continue steering clear of one another after that point. Anytime we were in close proximity, it always ended the same."

Before Ben left for the night, Chelsea pieced together most of the details that led to their demise, and despite not remembering it, felt a sadness gripping her from the whole situation. From the way he described everything, the two of them had been in love and were happy, and for it to all end over nothing more than a few stupid misunderstandings made her head and heart ache.

Chelsea always felt with her whole heart and had always been pretty hardheaded, so she could see where she might lose her temper. Though, honestly, a big part of her hoped she outgrew some of that in these recent months that she could no longer recall.

Other than asking him questions about their past, she really didn't know what to say to Benjamin, or Ben as he told her she could call him. It was an awkward situation. Ben was so unreadable it was a little irritating. He sounded like some historian reciting random facts, rather than the story of their lives. He told her the basic outline and gave her a few details of their time together, including how it all ended. Yet he came all the way out here when he heard she'd been in an accident. Not only that, but he also stayed the entire time, came to see her every day. Checked in on her, kept up the guise that they were still married to anyone who didn't know better just so he would know how she was. It was a lot of sacrifice for someone who wasn't in love.

Ben rarely showed emotion when they were alone. His handsome face was utterly void except for those hauntingly dark eyes of his. His voice had grown softer a time or two, and had more life in it when he spoke with a nurse or doctor, but when it was just the two of them, he almost sounded professional. Ben's timber was strong and smooth, a little clipped. She also noted that he seemed to avoid touching her at all costs. Though she wasn't sure if that was just her overreacting.

When she noticed the ring on his finger, she asked him if he had remarried. He told her no. Then, when he stood to leave, she also saw that it matched the very one the nurses returned to her.

Chapter Three

Chelsea couldn't stop smiling when she caught her first glimpse of familiar red hair through the sliver of a window on her hospital room door. She was damn near giddy when that door finally opened and Danielle's familiar face greeted her. The pair had been best friends since middle school and were nearly inseparable for most of their lives.

"Danny," Chelsea breathed out, tears welling up. Until that moment, she really didn't know how badly she needed to see a familiar face. The mousey redhead looked older, more mature than Chelsea recalled, but she was still the girl she'd always been. It took only one glance to know that.

Danielle wiped furiously at the tears in her own eyes but smiled bigger all the same as she fully stepped into the room. She didn't waste any time crossing the small space to where Chelsea was sitting. The two of them hugged and then hugged again.

"I am so happy to see you," Danielle said, positively beaming.

Just then, a few more familiar faces appeared in the doorway. Holly Carlisle and Nate Stevens, two of her other closest friends. Holly had always been stop-you-dead-in-your-tracks beautiful, and the past few years had obviously been more than kind to her. Chelsea could count on one hand how many times she'd ever seen the busty brunette looking anything less than perfect. Out of everyone, she would point fingers toward Nate for being the most surprising revelation. It wasn't as though he looked bad, just that he had changed the most from where her memories left off.

"I'd tell you that you were looking good, but I wouldn't want to lie," Holly teased. The brunette gave Chelsea a long once over. "It is nice to see Sleeping Beauty is awake," she offered with a smile. All teeth. All Holly.

Behind her was Nate, rolling his eyes. "You always know just what to say, Holl."

"What? I think we can all see she looks like a train wreck," Holly said. "Not that she can't be fixed with a little time and some good makeup, of course."

Danielle shook her head, her long hair falling around her thin shoulders. "Just put the flowers and balloons over there on the windowsill and sit down, will you?"

Chelsea couldn't help but laugh as they all fell into a cycle of conversation. This was the most normal she had felt since she woke up. There were obvious changes amongst their group since her last memory of them, but it felt so, so nice to have them here. She might even say it was close to normal.

"So, how are you feeling?" Danielle asked after everyone got a bit more settled. "I mean, really? It sounds like it was a horrible ordeal you went through."

"Lost. For starters." Chelsea shrugged. "Physically, I'm unnaturally sore most of the time, which has limited what I can do and made me rather antsy. Emotionally, I'm drained, beyond confused. I have this whole life that I can't remember a single moment of."

"Like Benny Boy?" Nate asked.

"Don't you start," both Holly and Danielle said in unison. To which Nate huffed out a breath, his lean arms crossing in front of his chest.

"Yeah, he is certainly one thing throwing me for a loop," Chelsea said. "You hear about these types of things happening all the time, but I don't think it's possible to really grasp what it's like until you're the one experiencing it firsthand."

Danielle reached over and gently squeezed her hand. "Ben said that the last thing you could remember was back in our freshman year of college?"

Chelsea nodded. "It was sometime around that week you failed your first psych test."

"Okay, wow." Nate said. "That seems like a lifetime ago."

"Not to me," Chelsea said quietly, earning sympathetic looks from the others. But then she smiled brightly. "So, who wants to start catching me up?"

The foursome spent the entire day together, and Chelsea couldn't have been happier. They didn't stay in her room much. Danielle wheeled her around the floors. They ate in the cafe area Ben mentioned the night before. She even got to go outside and breathe some fresh air. It was a bit of a task with the few tubes still hooked up to her, but well worth the small annoyance.

The small gang made her laugh so hard she cried, discussing embarrassing moments from high school, memories that would last a lifetime. Memories she was never more thankful to have intact. "Oh my gosh," Danielle said, leaning closer. "Do you remember that night my parents caught us sneaking out?"

They didn't just fill Chelsea in on her own life. They discussed Nate and Holly and how the two of them grew into the couple they were. Danny told her all about Saltridge and what was going on around the town she missed so much. They also caught her up on some of the bigger newsworthy stories from the area over the last several years. Who went and got themselves arrested, who had up and moved away, a few big storms that passed through, and all the little details only she would find interesting. Like, how the video store she loved so much went out of business the year prior.

Holly and Nate were back and forth with their relationship in high school, and Chelsea remembered their split after graduation. Holly left Saltridge behind to make a big name for herself in Los Angeles. She was going to be a star, or so she thought at age nineteen.

The image of Nate moping around all heartbroken over Holly was still fresh in Chelsea's mind. Hopefully, they could make it work this time.

Not having been one for school, Nate decided against going to college and instead joined an array of part-time jobs after high school ended. He seemed to have found his calling in home renovation with his great-uncle up there in the mountains, though. He looked grown up, maybe more than any of them these days, and he sure beamed whenever they discussed anything about Holly.

Nate and Holly weren't the only ones with surprising news. Danielle graduated with a degree in art history and had found a love for traveling. She shared a few of her adventures, including all the details from her latest cruise.

The mousey redhead had really grown into her own.

Chelsea learned that she and her boyfriend Oliver split up after he made a mistake with another girl, how it wrecked her best friend for a long time after. While Oliver left Saltridge to focus on his music, Danielle moved on, falling in love with a girl named Penny Swanson.

Danielle also brought Chelsea some pictures, a few albums, in fact. She skimmed through them, everyone pointing at different photos and telling her what was going on in each, but she didn't have the mental strength to fully go through them just yet.

It wasn't until morning that Chelsea picked up the items Danielle left, flipping through the old letters and photos. There were a lot of familiar faces in the album, along with plenty she didn't recognize.

What stood out to her the most were a few photos of her and Ben. There weren't many, and they were buried at the back of the album. She sucked in a breath at her first glimpse of the two of them together.

She couldn't look away. They looked so happy. So in love.

Chelsea carefully traced the outline of the photograph. She could practically feel how much adoration the two people in this photo had for one another. Ben didn't look anything like the stoic man who had been keeping her company. He was so relaxed in every picture, always smiling and holding onto her as if his whole world might slip away.

Chelsea was so caught up in the photographs that she didn't realize she was crying until a big fat tear plunked down on the page in front of her. She also didn't realize the man helping cause these powerful emotions was back in her room.

"Chelsea?" Ben asked. "You okay?"

Chelsea jumped at his deep voice, hurriedly wiping her eyes.

He would choose now to show up. Right when she never looked more ridiculous. Leave it to her to have an emotional breakdown over a relationship and a man she didn't even remember. Danielle would love hearing about this. Even more so now that her heart was pounding at the mere sight of him standing there.

She had missed him.

Which was utterly and completely ridiculous.

She sighed. Her cheeks were warm, and she didn't need a mirror to know that she was blushing something furious. "Yes. Just a touch emotional, it seems."

He gave her one of his infamous tight smiles before looking further around the room. "What do you have there?" he asked, nodding toward the pile in her lap.

Her cheeks grew warmer. "Oh, um, Danielle brought me some photos and stuff yesterday. They thought they might help fill me in on those lost years, see if anything jogged my memory."

"Smart idea," he said, leaning back against the wall behind him.

"Is it working?"

Chelsea shook her head. "No, not really. I mean, I've had a mix of emotions looking at a few of them, but I don't really know if that's because I'm remembering something about the photo itself, or just overflow from my dumpster fire of a life."

Ben almost smiled. "Those memories will return. You just have to give it time."

"I hope so. That's pretty much the go-to line everyone keeps throwing at me, anyway."

His large hands slid into his jean's pockets.

"Are you going to sit down?"

"No," he said, shaking his head. "I'm only staying for a few minutes."

"Oh?"

Ben tilted his head, and her throat tightened at the first real sign of emotion. It was gone in a blink, but she caught it. Only a second or two before that stony look fell back into place, Ben cleared his throat and looked down at his feet, which were covered in the same expensive-looking sneakers he usually wore.

"I should go. Danielle and the others will probably be here soon."

So, that's why he was missing yesterday. He didn't want to see her friends.

Ben almost made it out the door a second time, but before he could get there, the trio bounded in. Tension quickly filled the air as Nate, Holly and Danielle entered and noticed her ex-husband standing there.

Chelsea watched as the most important people in her life collided.

"Hey Danny." Ben nodded politely to her best friend, who smiled and stepped forward, embracing him in a quick hug. Holly only waved. Nate was a different story, getting annoyed at the mere sight of the other man.

"What the hell is he doing here?"

Ben ignored him at first, again stating that he was heading out. But Nate didn't seem to take anyone's hint. "Chelsea has friends here now. People that care about her. You know, in case there's somewhere you would rather be…"

"Just because I took her shit does not mean I'm going to take yours now," Ben growled, making his way to the door. The two men stared one another down for several tense moments before Ben slipped back outside.

Chelsea waited for the room to fall silent. "Okay. Who wants to explain?"

Ben cursed under his breath as he charged through the parking garage. Fuck Nate Stevens. He should have left when he had the chance. He never saw eye to eye with that asshole, but somewhere in between their first meeting and his split with Chelsea, they learned to tolerate one another. Then, when everything went to hell, well, all bets were off. Thankfully, he'd been able to avoid the fucker since.

Of all the problems in the world, Nathanial Stevens was not on the top of his list to waste time or effort on.

Danielle was another story. She wasn't exactly on his team when shit hit the fan, but she always tried to keep some sort of peace between them. Not that it did much good. But something shifted with Chelsea's accident. Once he got in contact with her regarding his ex-wife, they wound up lost in an hours' long conversation about Chelsea and his life since the divorce. Ben finally told her his side of what led him to those fateful decisions.

Danielle couldn't believe it. Some days he couldn't, either.

Not that it mattered much at this point.

Chelsea had another fun-filled day with her friends. Holly and Nate left before Danielle since they had an earlier flight to catch. She hated to see them go, but knew they had their own lives to get back to. While she adored the other couple, she was growing tired of Nate's attitude anytime she mentioned Ben. She also didn't mind a bit of one-on-one time with her best friend.

Chelsea sighed. "Do you know what I'm doing in Texas?" Ben hadn't known. If there was anyone who could provide some insight, it was Danielle.

Danielle nodded. "I also know why you were leaving. You know, when the accident happened."

Chapter Four

The day was on its way to a close when Ben finally showed up. The hospital's strict policy regarding visiting hours had Chelsea worried that she wouldn't see him at all. Danielle had left hours ago and while she appreciated the rest, she had grown rather lonely in the hours she had to herself.

"Chelsea," Ben greeted upon entering the room.

"What's all that?" she asked.

Ben walked over, putting the white carryout container on her bedside table first. She could have damn near kissed him for that alone. She was starving. Breakfast had been decent, but lunch and dinner had been quite a letdown. Sure, she could have gone to the cafe now that she knew where it was, but that would have required her to go downstairs, and she didn't want to miss Ben coming by, stupid as that might be.

"Thank you," Chelsea said, sliding the tray closer to have a look at her new goodies. A Greek salad had never looked better.

He shrugged. "If there's anything particular you want me to get, just let me know. Like I said, there's a pretty good selection downstairs and there's a ton of restaurants around here so, it's no trouble."

"Thank you," she said just before taking her first bite. "I might just take you up on that."

"Please do." Ben then lifted his other hand, which was still holding a few bags. "I got you a few things while I was out," he told her, gently laying the plastic bags on the bed. "Your cellphone got destroyed in the accident, so I got you a new one. I added a couple of numbers that you might need, including mine. There are a few books by a romance novelist you used to like, some of those gossip rags you liked to read and pretend you didn't."

He flashed her a quick smile, and her heart skipped another beat. He should do that more often. Dark and mysterious was overrated.

"There are some toiletry items you might need," he said. "I know hospitals don't have the greatest selection. There's still some stuff out in the car. I'll be right back."

He spun and walked back out the door before she could say anything to stop him. Not that she had any idea what she was supposed to say. Or how she was ever supposed to repay him for everything he was doing.

While keeping one hand on her food tray, Chelsea grabbed for the closest bag she could reach. Like he promised, she found a couple of magazines, a handful of books, even a crossword and a new set of pens. All things she was especially thankful for, since she still wasn't sure when they planned on releasing her.

The other bags contained everything from a bottle of shampoo and another of conditioner, both her favorite brands.

Body wash, a shower poof, and even a box of tampons. She warmed at the idea of this large slab of a man going through a store and grabbing all these fruit and flower-scented items for her.

When he returned, those muscled arms of his were holding several more bags. Ben cleared his throat as he straightened back up. "There are some clothes and a couple pairs of shoes," he told her, putting his hands in his pockets. Today he was wearing nice dress shoes, black pants and a nice black pull-over. His hair was a little damp from the rain pounding outside the window.

Chelsea moved her leg, nearly knocking over the last bag, one that she hadn't gotten to yet. The one with the cell phone in it.

"Shit!" She leaned forward much quicker than she should have. The world rolled by in a giant wave as a sharp pain shot through the base of her skull.

Ben was there in no time, using those long legs of his to round the bed and grab the small bag before it could fall off and hit the hard ground.

"What's wrong?" he asked next, his hand touching her leg.

Chelsea swallowed hard; her pain momentarily forgotten as she focused on the sensation. "Hmm? Oh, nothing," she said. "Just moved a little too quickly."

Ben's hand snapped back to his side. "How are you feeling today?"

Chelsea frowned. "Not the worst, considering. Nate and Holly had to take off early to catch their flight, so there was some time for just me and Danny." She surveyed him. "You look tired."

"Is that your way of saying I look like shit?"

Chelsea's cheeks lit on fire. His tone hadn't changed, but there was something about the way he said it. He gave her a hint of a smile before and now he was being all snippety… without the snip.

Before she could pull her foot out of her mouth, he sighed. "I've had a long day."

"How so?" Chelsea asked once her heartbeat steadied. She knew he lived states away and seemed to have a pretty important job. She hated that he was missing so much because of her. "I hope it's not work related."

He waved that thought right off. "I can't leave you like this."

"Danielle filled me in on what I was doing out here. In Texas, I mean."

He was preparing to leave, but she didn't want to let him go just yet.

Ben's eyes met hers. "Well. That's good."

Chelsea hated the simple way he said that. Why couldn't he pry like every other man on the planet? "She said I went to stay with her and Penny for a few weeks after I left Saltridge. Apparently, the two of us had some sort of big blow-out?"

He nodded, but quickly looked away again.

"I went there to figure out what I wanted to do next. She said it kind of dawned on me that I needed a new start in order to get past everything with us. So, when I got a job offer out here, I jumped at the chance."

Ben nodded, repeating his previous statement.

Chelsea continued on, telling him what little she knew about the move and the job she took, and how things were going as far as the redhead knew. It sounded lonely, but according to Danielle, she had been enjoying some aspects of this new Texas adventure.

Chelsea bit her lip when he remained silent. If only she could read his mind. She kept the rest of what Danielle said to herself, especially the part leading up to her car wreck. Why she was so far from her new home. Where she was going.

It wasn't like there was anything to gain by telling him.

"I think you were going to see him when the crash happened," Danielle told her.

"Going to see him? Who? Ben?" Chelsea's eyes widened.

Danielle nodded. "I think so."

Danielle went on to explain that she got what she wanted when she fled the state of California. She hadn't heard from Ben and had finally calmed down because of it. And she had confessed to her best friend that she actually missed him. Just a day or so before the accident took place, she gave Danielle the impression that she was going back to talk to Ben.

Not that she could tell him that. Not when it was bound to stir up emotions in both of them. Ones that she wouldn't even be able to comprehend. It's not like she could answer his questions or reassure him about anything in her current state.

Whatever intentions she had back then were just as lost as she was.

Chelsea waited until Ben left to pull herself out of bed and go over to the bags of clothes he left. A nurse popped her head in to check her vitals only a few minutes later, whistling at the scene and commenting on how lucky she must be to have a husband like that.

She was lucky to have him. Even if he wasn't her husband anymore.

It did not surprise Chelsea to find quite the array of clothing after seeing the number of bags Ben brought in. Carefully, she pulled each item out and removed the tags. She wouldn't need anything for a while. This ex-husband of hers had her style down to a science.

Chelsea was chatting with Olivia at the nurse's station when Ben came walking down the hall.

"Your wife got all dolled up today."

Ben smiled. "I see that," he said, looking her over. "Even all bruised up, you are still the most beautiful woman I have ever seen."

Ben's eyes softened the longer he stared. He made her feel more exposed than any doctor or hospital ever could.

But the trance only lasted so long. In the next breath, she blinked, and he snapped back out of it.

Ben kept an eye on her as they walked through the

halls, but seemed to look anywhere else once they were in the elevator. He kept a close enough distance to grab her if she faltered but left plenty of space between them.

"So," she said once they were seated near the deli. "Tell me something about yourself, Mister Black."

Ben's thumb froze over his phone screen. "It might be best if you focus more on answers about yourself."

"Finding out more about you is learning about myself, is it not? Obviously, we shared a life together. So you are currently the expert on everything I lost. And that says a lot about me. Who I fell in love with, what we shared." At his subtle glare, she added, "Besides, I can't say I'm not simply just a little curious."

Ben briefly ran her through some of the important things. She learned that his mother was a librarian and his father an engineer. Ben touched on his mother's long battle with cancer, and how it was too much for his father's heart to handle. Chelsea's dad took off when she was two, but she barely survived her mother's death. She couldn't imagine burying both of your parents so close together.

"Did I know them?"

"My parents? Yes. You and my mother were thick as thieves whenever you got together."

Ben told her about how he left for Boston after high school ended. He graduated two years early, so moving away to college had been a bit of a challenge. But he had enjoyed it, and his parents were both proud of him.

He described a few jobs that he held over the years, then how he later landed one at Waterstone after getting his first degree. He left Boston for New York and seemed to have really enjoyed his years there. Chelsea couldn't remember ever having been to the Big Apple, but Ben told her they had made a few trips together.

She already knew he moved to Los Angeles for the job at Waterstone and how they met, but Ben told her more about the company and his role. He even divulged some more information about the two of them, which had her hanging onto every word.

"Did you have many relationships before me?" she asked. She could only remember a handful of guys that she dated in high school and then Ian her freshman year. She was sure with his looks he had to have women fawning over him, and even now the idea filled her with jealousy.

One of his hands came up to rub the back of his neck. "I wouldn't exactly say they were relationships…"

"A lot of one-night stands?"

"There were some flings. I dated casually, and sometimes, yes, less than that. The closest thing I had to an actual relationship lasted six or seven months. I wasn't the type to settle down."

"What happened?"

Those soulful brown eyes looked up just as something inside of them stole her breath away. "You came along."

Chapter Five

Chelsea and Ben were both surprised by their guest the next day. The door opened and in walked a nicely built dark-haired stranger with piercing blue eyes. He wore an enormous cowboy hat and a pair of blue jeans that looked like they had been made specifically for him. "Howdy strangers," the man said after glancing at the two of them.

Chelsea didn't recognize him, but one glance at Ben revealed that he did. Ben looked surprised to see him, though. "Linds," Ben said as he got to his feet. "What in the world are you doing here?"

"I was passing through," this Linds person answered.

Ben paused. "Passing through?"

"Mm-hmm," he answered with a smirk. Those blue eyes flickered back to Chelsea, and he smiled brightly. He was all teeth and charm. "How you doin' there, sweetheart?"

Before she could answer, Ben turned to look at her. "Chelsea, this is Lindsey Macintyre. He's an old friend of mine."

Lindsey nodded toward her.

"Oh. Well, um, hi there. I'm doing as well as can be expected, I suppose. How are you?"

"I am doing just fine. Thank you," he answered, those pretty eyes sparkling, a smile still on his face. "I hear you had quite the ordeal. And from the looks of it, you still have some holes there in your memory?"

Chelsea nodded. "More like one big, endless one."

"Don't you worry. The brain's a funny thing, sometimes it just needs time to get itself all sorted back out. I'm sure you'll be back to your old self soon enough."

"I hope so."

Lindsey stole a glance over at Ben before crossing his legs and leaning against the counter. "I must say, for a woman who got hit by two semis and a minivan before rolling off into a ditch, you are looking mighty fine."

Chelsea blushed, lowering her head to look at her hands. "Thank you. I've been told I got very lucky." When he didn't reply, Chelsea lifted her head back up to find Lindsey and Ben staring at one another. "E-everything okay?"

Lindsey laughed. "Just go sit down," he said to Ben. Then he looked back at Chelsea. "Don't mind him. Ben gets overly jealous when it comes to you. You might not remember this, but the first time you and I met Ben here, up and punched me right in the face. Damn near broke my nose. Had a black eye for weeks."

"You deserved it."

"Hey, all I did was compliment a beautiful woman."

"You were looking down the front of her dress!"

"While giving her a compliment!"

Ben shook his head.

Lindsey laughed heartily.

Chelsea only smiled as the pair went back and forth. Ben seemed more relaxed with his friend here. Once the two of them took a seat, Ben went back to his usual chair while Lindsey jumped up to sit on the counter beside the sink.

"You behind his angry southern drawl?"

Lindsey whistled. "Only when he curses. So you have heard it?"

"Just the once."

Lindsey laughed at that. "He got me back for that, too, believe me. I turn into an angry Irishman whenever I have more than my fair share of alcohol. Or if I get really mad. Or a combination of the two. And trust me, that freaks everyone out more than anything else."

Chelsea didn't want to go when a nurse appeared to take her to another floor. Unfortunately, she didn't have a choice in the matter.

Both men stood, Lindsey reaching out a hand to her. "In case I don't see you before I take off, I just want to say it was nice seeing you again, and I wish you a speedy recovery. You take care now," he said just before Olivia wheeled her away. "Now come on, Benjamin," Chelsea heard from down the hall. "You can buy me lunch."

Lindsey waited for the waitress to leave their menus. "I see you're still in love with her. How's that workin' out?"

Ben sighed, then reached over to take a drink of water. "What are you doing here, Linds? Really."

Lindsey let out a deep breath as he relaxed against the high-backed booth. "I came to check up on you, see how you were holding up. This can't be easy on you."

"I appreciate the concern."

"Hey, you can try and hide it all you want, but I know better," Lindsey said, finishing just as the waitress came over to get their orders. "The suits must be missing you."

Ben shrugged. "I've been in touch with them just about every day. Mostly been doing things from my cell phone or laptop. Think I'll have to go back for a few days near the end of next week, though."

"Can't say I was surprised by you deciding to stay out here with her."

"She was fucking unconscious," Ben said after a moment. "Then, when she woke up." He paused. "It's one thing to be stuck in the hospital, another to be stuck in the hospital and have a good chunk of your memory missing."

Lindsey huffed out a little laugh. "Whether she woke up with her memory intact or not, you would have stayed out here until she was released. We both know that. She could have woken up, spotted you. Told you to go fuck yourself. As she's done many times. And you would still be here. Maybe not being all buddy-buddy in her room, but your love struck dumbass would be checking up on her in some way."

Ben sighed. The man wasn't wrong.

The waitress came back to see if they were ready to

order, and after a few more minutes, they finally let her know what they wanted.

"Maybe the universe is throwing you a bone, taking her memories away like that."

Ben raised an eyebrow. "What do you mean?"

Lindsey shrugged his shoulders. "Maybe this is that second chance you always wanted. A way to make her fall in love with you all over again."

Ben snorted. "I don't think it works like that, Linds."

"Why not? Looks to me like you got a fresh start right in front of you."

"Yeah... Until those memories do come back. And then what? It's going to be a shitstorm all over again. Chelsea's going to raise absolute hell over me even being here in the first place. It will be nothing more than manipulation as far as she's concerned, taking advantage of the circumstances."

Ben reached up to rub his eyes as they gathered their things to head out.

"And I really don't need that."

Lindsey leaned against the door to his truck. The weather seemed to be taking the turn the meteorologist promised. It couldn't be more than a couple of degrees above freezing. The night was going to be a cold one.

"Don't you need to get on the road?"

Lindsey blew out a heavy sigh. "I have never seen two people more in love than you and Chelsea were. And I've never seen anyone more ignorant, either, to let it go like you did."

Ben smirked. "Well, you couldn't have one without the other."

"Mr. Black," Chelsea's morning nurse greeted. "You're here just in time."

Ben raised an eyebrow while Chelsea looked mortified. "In time for what?"

"The doctor cleared your wife for a shower. I was going to stand in there to make sure she didn't fall, but now that you're here." The young nurse smiled.

Ben cleared his throat. "I don't think that's the best idea. You're as much of a stranger as I am right now."

"Oh nonsense," she said, her hand waving through the air. Then, before he or Chelsea could discuss the situation any further, they were left alone.

Ben sighed, rubbing a hand down his face. "Come on," he said. "I'll keep my back turned. I'll only be there if you need me. Okay?"

Chelsea hesitated, but passing up a shower was not on her to-do list. Besides, it wasn't like there was anything he hadn't already seen.

As promised, Ben wasted no time turning and looking at the door. Nevertheless, Chelsea turned her own back to his as she undressed, her fingers slightly shaking. "Where's your partner in crime?"

"Lindsey lives a few hours north. In Oklahoma. He stopped by on his way home."

Chelsea turned the water on. It wasn't going to be anywhere near the hot temperatures she remembered at home, but it beat a sponge bath. Chelsea tilted her head back and closed her eyes as water rained down her aching body. Other than her head injury, most of her wounds had healed. Though there were still a few tender spots that stung as she stood there.

After rinsing out her hair and gently lathering up with the body wash Ben brought her, Chelsea snuck a glance at the man in question. He hadn't moved. Ben looked extra delicious today for some reason, standing there in his dark jeans and tight black t-shirt. There was some sort of design peeking beneath his brown leather jacket.

"Can I ask you something?"

"Hmm?" he asked, tilting his head to the side the tiniest bit.

"About Veronica."

Ben went stiff but stayed silent. Chelsea held her hands over her breasts, squeezing the loofah. "You mentioned that she was a friend?"

Ben slid his hands into his pockets. He was silent for a long time. "Not friends so much," he said, then cleared his throat. "But we did know one another."

Chelsea waited for him to gather his thoughts as she continued to enjoy the warm water. There was something about that woman's name that gave her chills.

"We met in college. Veronica was a few years older than me, but we had a couple of classes together and several friends in common, so our paths crossed more than a few times." Chelsea thought she heard him swallow. "Veronica Craft was—is—the heiress to a digital securities company. The first of its kind. Her father wouldn't let her join the company officially until she got an education. We were never close. There was never a relationship there, but yes, we did know one another."

Ben shuffled his feet and continued, "After she graduated, she left to go run part of her father's company. I would get a mass email from her from time to time, but that was it. I might have replied to one, I think. When Waterstone implemented new systems, they put in a bid and suddenly Veronica, her father and a few others from their company were hovering around the office."

"Why you? What made Veronica target us?"

Ben sighed loudly. "I don't really know," he said, reaching up to rub his neck. "I mean, she showed an interest in me back in school, but it was never reciprocated. We remained friendly enough when we saw one another, so I never thought much of it. Then, she fell out of my life for all those years, and life went on. I met you, and we started our life together. I guess she was jealous. You had a bad feeling about her right from the start, but I just wasn't paying attention. You and her exchanged words a few times. I always took your side. But it wasn't enough. It didn't calm your fears, and it didn't get her to give it up, either."

Chelsea turned the water off, wrapped herself up in a towel, and quietly stepped out of the shower. This woman sounded insane.

Ben took a step forward, his hand reaching for the knob, but he paused.

"Veronica hacked into my email accounts and added some damning evidence that pointed towards us having an affair. Our tech guys sifted through it until they proved it was her. But it was too late. And the night—that night—I wasn't there with her. She wasn't even supposed to be there. I was in meetings all day and went back to the room to wait for you. I ordered some food, set out some swimwear so we could go laze around in the pool. I jumped in the shower while I was waiting. Hell, I called you just before I went to the bathroom to see where you were. I still don't know how everything got so fucked up."

"Is that snow?" Chelsea asked once Ben reappeared.

One of his large hands came up, brushing at his wide shoulders, then rubbing at his hair. "Yeah," he said. "It's coming down like freaking crazy out there."

Chelsea's eyes went wide. She didn't exactly put snow and Texas together and mentioned that to him. She glanced toward her window and felt a thrill go through her, a smile easily taking over her face.

Ben grumbled. "Yeah, well, locals seem to have the same thoughts as you from the way they all forgot how to drive at the first sight of a snowflake."

Chelsea laughed. "Wait right there," she told him, hurrying to the bathroom. She threw on a hoodie and switched out her slippers for sneakers in a rush. "Come on," she said, already heading toward the hall. "Do you think they'd let me go out in it?"

"I highly doubt it," Ben said, following behind her. "I can ask?"

Chelsea didn't answer. Instead, she led him down a few hallways, a quick ride in the elevator, and then down to where a set of doors led outside.

"Chels?"

She just smiled, wasting no time before stepping out into the cold air and opening her arms out wide as the white fluff rained down. She laughed, spinning around.

When she glanced back, all the air rushed out of her.

"You stay out here long enough and you're going to turn into a snowman. Snow... woman?" Ben told her, a big smile on his face, his nose bright red from the cold.

Chelsea stopped, forcing herself to take a breath. The cold air rushed through her, burning her lungs. She closed her eyes, the top half of her body leaning forward as she braced her hands on her knees.

"Chelsea?" she heard Ben shout, his worry evident. "Chels?" he called again when he reached her. "Are you okay? Come back inside."

"You told me I was going to turn into a snowman," she whispered.

"What?" he asked, his forehead scrunching up in confusion. He guided her over to a bench, sitting her down and kneeling before her. "Are you okay?"

She nodded slowly. "I think I remembered something."

His head tilted, eyes searching her face. "Come back inside and we'll tell your nurse, okay?"

She nodded, letting him lead her back inside and back to her floor.

"What happened?" Olivia asked her once they were back in her room.

Chelsea rubbed her arms. "I went outside and when I looked back to where Ben was standing, I don't know. Suddenly a feeling ripped through me. It was like a movie scene in my head."

"Well, what was it?"

Chelsea closed her eyes. "It was snowing. I don't know where we were, but Ben was standing in front of a big red door, and there was a bird feeder. It was shaped like a Christmas tree."

Olivia turned to Ben. "Do you remember anything like that?"

Ben shrugged. "I don't remember the exact conversation. But it sounds like she's describing Holly and Nate's house. We went up there for Christmas the year after we got married. They lived in a pretty isolated area, brick house, red door. Chelsea had been so excited by the storm; I could hardly keep her inside."

"Well, isn't this just a great bit of news? I'll let your doctor know. Is there anything else that you remember? Anything at all?"

Chelsea closed her eyes. She could hear Ben's laugh. Almost felt the sting of the snow between her toes. The door. The birdfeeder. His long jacket. But that was it. It didn't matter how hard she tried, there was nothing else. "No," she said, shaking her head. "But this is good, right?"

Olivia smiled. "It's a start."

Chapter Six

"Home?" Chelsea repeated. How could they send her home? "I don't even know where the hell that is!" She had only one other flash of a memory since her episode in the snow. She loathed any building that inhabited a medical professional, but she was far from ready to leave the sanctuary of these walls.

Chelsea's hands shook as she finished getting dressed. She fixed her hair into a loose ponytail, put on some light makeup and massaged a handful of lotion down her arms and thighs.

Her room was almost entirely bare, Ben having taken most of her things out to his car while she was getting ready. She was no longer hooked up to any machine, no tubes running to her veins, no white patient ID bracelet on her wrist, nor its red allergy alert twin.

"You want me to tell them we're ready?" Ben asked.

Chelsea only nodded.

"Okay," he said softly, stepping out into the hallway. "I'll go get the car pulled around."

The hours it took to get from the hospital to the apartment complex Chelsea was using as her current address felt never ending. They stopped at a drive-thru to eat but mostly stayed on the road. Ben kept the radio volume low while he shared a few stories of trips the two of them had taken in their years as a couple.

"Do you recognize any of this?" Ben asked once they were close to her complex.

"No." Nothing was familiar. Not the apartments themselves or the surrounding area.

Ben's eyes held the silent question as she went inside to look around the space. The apartment was a decent size but didn't look very lived in. The living room held a matching tan couch and loveseat. There was a small bookshelf which was entirely filled, and a desk with a computer and chair in one corner.

The kitchen was small but there were new appliances inside. A list from her landlord sat on the counter describing the items that were to remain. The hallway was bare. Not a single picture hung. Her full-sized bed was messy and unmade. A ceiling fan hung above it. She had a laptop laid out on the bed and a tall standing lamp in one corner of the room.

"I was really hoping coming here would be like turning a key in a lock," she said softly. "That I would suddenly remember at least some of it."

Ben nodded. "I'm sorry, Chels."

Ben wasn't surprised by Chelsea's bare apartment. Thanks to Danielle he knew most of her things were still sitting back at the house in Saltridge. She hadn't taken much with her when she hightailed it out of the small California town. It was hard to imagine her here. Chelsea's presence wasn't exactly felt around the place. The colors weren't hers, nor was the lack of decor and random things she would up and buy and string about everywhere. The walls were bare, with not even one of her prized possessions to be seen.

Ben sighed as he tossed what used to be a head of lettuce into the trash.

"Bag for the car is packed," Chelsea said, coming up beside him. "And I found a flier for some Chinese place. Anything particular you want?"

"You sure you got everything?"

Chelsea shrugged. "Only one way to find out. Here," she said, passing him the flier. "My treat. No arguments."

The sun had long since set by the time the food arrived and they finished eating. So, when a knock sounded at the door both of them jerked around in surprise.

Chelsea paled as she stepped to open it. "Who could that be?"

"Oh, Jesus, Chelsea. You look like death decided to give you a warning."

Ben blew out a breath. Thank fucking God the voice was feminine, and very Texan.

"Oh, Lord, I'm sorry," the girl said, taking another step closer. "I was told you lost some of your memory and here I am probably freaking you out more. My name's Emilia Brighton, you can call me Emily. I live right next door."

"Oh," Chelsea said, glancing quickly at her. "Oh, I'm so sorry. Would you like to come in?"

This Emily woman was slender. She had long, wildly curly hair that looked like it weighed as much as the rest of her put together. "I didn't know you already had company," Emily said once she spotted him. "You're Benjamin?"

"Um, yes… I am."

Emily continued to stare. "Somehow you look even better in person," she said. "I wouldn't have thought that possible."

"Uh, thanks?"

Emily shook her head. "Sorry. Chelsea showed me some pictures of you. And just wow. Okay, anyway. Chelsea! I wanted to see if there was anything I could help you out with? Anything you might need?"

"Oh, I think we're fine," Chelsea said with another glance his way. "We're actually only here for the night."

"Well, if you run into any hiccups feel free to come knock on my door. I sure am going to miss you. Perhaps we can reconnect once your head gets all healed up."

Chelsea nodded. "Perhaps."

"She seemed nice."

"Yeah, maybe? Makes me wish I could remember her." Chelsea sighed and plopped down on the couch. "Sometimes it's not so bad, you know. Not remembering. But times like that sure make me feel like I'm drowning under it all."

"Remember," Ben said, leaning closer. "We remodeled."

Chelsea inhaled the crisp California air. He was right. The streets of Saltridge had changed, but it still felt like home.

Felt like her.

Chelsea went inside while Ben grabbed her things from his car. Ben warned her it would look different inside, and he certainly hadn't lied. She stood in the foyer, gazing around the house. The flooring was all new, even the hardwood. The walls were a different color than she remembered and there were several built-in storage shelves that she didn't recall. Everything was a bit brighter than her mother would have liked, but it was beautiful.

She moved out of the way when Ben came in. "What do you think?" he asked as he set her bags next to the stairs.

Chelsea turned from the photograph she was admiring. "It's going to take some getting used to. I like it. It's just-"

"Different?"

She nodded. "Yeah."

Chelsea continued walking room by room. The light gray and white walls were welcoming. When she got to the dining room, she paused. "Ben?" she called out. "Was this room red at one time?"

He stared at her for a minute. "Yeah. You were thinking about going with a different color scheme at first. You thought you wanted to go a little bolder, dark reds and grays."

Chelsea reached for the simple silver string necklace she had around her neck and grasped at her wedding ring that strung on it. "I think I remember the swatches on that wall," she said, pointing a finger.

"You painted the living room and had started on the kitchen. I think you got half of the wall done before you changed your mind. Gregory's wife gave you that yellow and white rug down in the living room when they moved to England, and you changed your whole idea about the house from there."

He laughed at her grimace. "You only just started, so it wasn't that big of a deal. You waited to buy the new furniture and stuff until after the floors and walls and cabinets were all done."

Chelsea could tell the house was well lived in and very loved. It was sad to think of it sitting empty while she was gone for all those months.

It was easier to spot the home's missing pieces upstairs. Large gaping empty holes on the wall. A shelf that shouldn't be bare, indents on the carpet from furniture she couldn't remember.

Did Ben's new home hold these same ghosts? She supposed not. He told her that he was renting a place in the city. His place didn't have any empty spots to fill.

The guest bedroom she knew was suspiciously bare. It appeared to have been converted to an office, and even almost empty, it felt like Ben. Her old bedroom was now the one for guests. Somehow, it felt smaller as she stood in the middle of the room.

The last bedroom, her mother's, had become theirs. Or rather, hers.

As Chelsea stepped a few feet into the room, something struck her.

One of Ben's hands tangled in her hair as their lips collided, the other held her close, gently pushing her bottom against him. She already lost her dress and heels. She was standing before him in nothing but her lacy black bra.

"You are wearing far too much clothing," she pouted, reaching for his tie.

"You know," he said, his voice husky as he lifted her up into the air, wrapping her legs around him. "I couldn't agree more." She smiled wide when those heavy hands slid from her foot to her ankle, and up to her knee before seeking warmer ground. "You're still wearing too many clothes."

Ben smirked. There was no rush in pulling his hands away from her soft flesh. He purposely took even longer taking off his tie and working the buttons of his shirt.

"I guess we'll just have to fix that."

Chelsea jumped at the knock on the open bedroom door. Her face went up in flames when Ben popped his head inside.

"Hey, I was—are you alright?"

"Hmm? Yes," she lied. It was entirely too warm.

Those dark eyes bore into her. "You sure? Did something happen?"

Apparently!

Thankfully, that didn't quite reach her mouth. She cleared her throat, trying her best not to look at him. Or think of him stripping in front of her, the way his lips felt, his body against hers. Or what might have happened next.

"N-no. Just feeling a bit overwhelmed." At least that wasn't an entire falsified statement.

He didn't look convinced but didn't call her out on it. "I was going to see if you wanted to head into town with me, but it might be best for you to stay here," he said slowly, his eyes never leaving her.

"Okay." While she didn't want him to leave, a little space wasn’t the worst idea.

"I'll be back in a little while. I thought I would go get you stocked up on some groceries and things. You have my number if you need anything."

She nodded.

"Anything you want me to pick up while I'm out?"

Chelsea shook her head. "Nothing I can think of."

"Alright," he said. "You going to be alright here by yourself?"

"I think so. I might start putting some of my things away."

"Okay. Well, there's no rush. I'll be back shortly."

Chelsea let out a hard and shaky breath once the front door closed. "Get a hold of yourself, woman."

Chapter Seven

Ben didn't intend to stay the night. Hell, he wasn't going to stay any longer than it took to get Chelsea groceries and whatever else she might need. But when she asked him to stay, there wasn't anything in the world that could have made him deny her simple request.

Instead of heading back to his apartment in Los Angeles, he cleaned up the house alongside her, made a few calls, and wound up ordering a few pizzas which sounded pretty damn good after the day they had.

Being around Chelsea was always a bit of a challenge, but now that they were back in their home, memories were flooding him at every turn.

Chelsea did most of the painting, but he and Nate installed new floors. He designed the storage features she wanted and helped install them. She had mostly been in charge of picking out the furniture, but he tagged along a few times. He moved every piece of furniture here a dozen times before she declared it perfect. His belongings, new and old, once had their places here, too.

And of course there were the memories. The good, the bad, and everything in between. He remembered the first time he walked through that front door just as well as the last. It wasn't easy being back here. The pain was raw, scratching at him endlessly.

The first time he saw Chelsea cry was in this house. He could still feel his thumbs on her face as he wiped away her salty, hot tears and rocked her in his arms. He carried her over that threshold as man and wife after saying their vows. Nearly died laughing in the foyer when a small bluebird got inside, and she went into a full-blown panic, screaming and ducking anytime it moved. He chased her up and down those stairs, all throughout the house many times when they were being extra playful with one another. The sitting room would be decked out in Christmas decorations once the holidays rolled around. Danielle gave her approval of him on the old couch there in the living room.

It was still with him. Every bit of it.

They were in love in this house. They made beautiful memories.

A good part of their falling apart and coming undone happened right here as well. She threw multiple items at him in the kitchen, in the bedroom. Screamed at him in every single room. He begged and pleaded for her to listen to him in the doorway of their bedroom before the first time she laid her hands on him, slapping him so hard his face kept the handprint she left for quite a while. She told him she hated him and never wanted to see him again from the middle of that staircase.

"What are you thinking about?"

"Nothing important." Neither of them missed the tiny hitch in his voice.

"I know it can't be easy on you being here," she said softly, looking down. "I am glad you stayed, though."

He shrugged, looking away before she could spot him.

When they walked into the living room, Chelsea went to the same spot she always did, and he studied her to see if it was due to a memory, but in the end, it seemed to be nothing more than a coincidence. He still thought she remembered something earlier before he went into town, but he wasn't going to push her on it. There were probably many things she wasn't going to want to share with anyone.

Especially him.

It took a few hours, and more than a couple glasses of wine, for Ben to relax. Chelsea stuck to her non-alcoholic sparkling juice but offered Ben some of the dark red substance. He turned her down at dinner but relented once she asked about their honeymoon.

Ben finished off the rest of the wine in his glass as he stood. "I think it's later than we both realize. If it's alright with you, I'm going to go upstairs to use the shower and then probably head on to bed."

Honestly, she didn't want the night to end, but she was a bit worn out herself. "That's fine. I told you earlier to make yourself at home."

Her words were awkward. This was his home. Their home.

Ben nodded. "Okay, well, I'll see you in the morning. Have a good night. I'm just down the hall if you need me."

She waited until he reached the stairs. "Ben?" He spun around. "Yeah?"

"If you could change one thing about us, what would it be?"

Long seconds ticked by. "If I could change one thing, I would change that we ever ended."

She looked away. "Well, that's a given, right?"

His head barely shook. "I don't mean it like that," he said softly. "I could say that if I could go back in time, I wouldn't have taken the promotion if that was what you wanted or even as just a precaution. Or refused to work as many hours. I could have sent Veronica and her father packing the second their feet touched Waterstone's floors. While I wish all or any of that were possible, if I had but one choice, one chance to change it my answer would be that I would change that we ever ended. Because all of that, it all could have still happened, but we still shouldn't have ended. We shouldn't be over, Chelsea."

"You feel that even now?"

He reached out and brushed a loose strand of hair out of her face then gave a sad smile. "Yes. Even after all the hell we put each other through. It was a mistake to give up on everything we had. We should have worked things out. Even now, hell, standing right here right now, I wish that things weren't over."

Before she could utter a single word, he was up the stairs. The soft click of the bathroom door echoing behind him.

Chelsea couldn't speak. Couldn't breathe.

How could something she didn't remember hurt so much?

Ben stood naked in front of the sink while the shower warmed up, tears threatening to leave the corners of his eyes.

He let out a long breath as he wiped them away. He had a miniscule buzz from the wine, just enough to make him a little fuzzy. It was almost nice.

He could blame his words on the wine, but that would be a lie. He knew what the tone behind her voice meant. He could see it in her eyes. He lived through her falling in love with him once, so it wasn't hard to spot the signs. It was screwing with his head as much as his heart. But he couldn't stop himself when she asked him that. He couldn't resist telling her in some small way that he still wanted her.

Chelsea turned around when the third car in half an hour slid across the road. There was no way she could make it all the way back home tonight, but there were a few motels a couple of miles back that had a vacancy sign.

"It's not like he's going anywhere," she said out loud to herself.

But what if?

Chelsea sighed as she attempted to smooth back her hair. She turned the radio up, hoping that it would distract her from her own thoughts long enough to get herself turned around.

Maybe she could use the extra time tonight to think about what she was going to say to him.

When the sign for the motel came into view, she blew out a sigh of relief. But within a matter of seconds that same sinking feeling returned. Her breath caught in her throat as the large, beaming headlights headed straight for her.

She screamed as her car collided with the semi. Her car slid across the hard cement and bounced off the median as though it was made of rubber. Chelsea watched in horror as the world outside blurred together in a smudge of concrete, metal, and clouds. Her car spun again and was just about to smash into a second truck when everything faded away.

"Chelsea!"

"Chelsea!" Someone shouted again, shaking her roughly.

The darkness gave way. Chelsea was trembling as she shot up in the bed. "Ben?"

He stood there, gripping her shoulders. He wasn't wearing a shirt. "Chelsea? Are you okay? You were screaming."

"I was?" she asked, rubbing her face. She could still feel the terror coursing through her veins from the crash. "Sorry."

He yawned then sat down beside her, one hand coming out to rest on her leg. "You want to talk about it?"

"I think it was the accident. Or the lead up to it, I guess. But I was in the car, worried about the other cars and the rain. I was going to pull over for the night." The fuzzy image from her dream was clearer now. "That's when it happened. Or at least started to. I remember watching, frozen, as the first truck hit and I slid across the highway. I was trying to stay calm, but then I sped up and there was another truck in front of me. I knew something bad was going to happen. I don't remember anything after that, just being terrified as I was about to get stuck between the two."

It happened in a breath. A blink. An instant. Ben's hands gripped her waist as he pulled her closer. She closed her eyes, breathing in the fresh smell of him, the warmth of his hard body. "I thought I was going to die. I wasn't ready."

Ben bent down, kissing the top of her head and nestling into her hair. "You're okay now," he whispered. "You're safe here."

"I feel safe with you."

Ben sighed but said nothing more, just held her. Chelsea was about to fall back asleep when he moved her, laying her back down and covering her up.

"Ben?"

"Hmm?"

"Stay with me? Please?"

He hesitated. "Chels, that's probably not the best idea."

"Please?"

Another sigh.

He rubbed his large hands down his tired face. "Yeah. Okay. Just give me a minute." And with that he walked out of the room. She heard him go into the bathroom and a few minutes later come back out.

Soon he was returning to her room with a blanket and pillow.

"You don't have to do that," she said when he tossed one of the blankets onto the floor.

"I really do," he said. "Go back to sleep. I'll be right here."

Chelsea watched him move around until he was comfortable. Then shifted herself into a better position. She wanted to crawl right down onto the floor and pretzel herself against him but just barely resisted the urge.

This time, when her eyes fell heavily, it was a nightmare-free slumber.

Over the weekend, Ben continued to help Chelsea settle in. He gave her one of his credit cards, and despite her many protests, deposited a large sum in her bank account. He made sure the house was stocked with any and everything she could think of. All of her bills were taken care of. Ben made sure to give her any numbers and addresses he thought she might need. From hospitals to restaurants, her friends' contact information as well as his own. It was all in preparation for him leaving. He had a job, his own place and life that he needed to get back to. He had been away for weeks, and he couldn't just babysit her until she remembered who she was. But that didn't mean she was ready for him to go.

He promised to come back on his days off, if she wanted, but that didn't seem like enough.

Several more memories also struck her. Nothing major, just small moments.

Chelsea remembered meeting Penny the first time and having a big party with her friends in the backyard. Being bored out of her mind, falling asleep on the couch on top of Ben. Gregory singing in some small coffee shop, leaving her speechless. There were also flashes of her in bed with some strange blonde man, but over her dead body was she bringing that up.

Chelsea picked at the polish on her nails. "What do you think is going to happen once my memories come back?"

Ben walked into the room and took a seat in the armchair closest to her. "I honestly don't know. But my guess? There's going to be a lot of yelling and cursing coming my way. And after that? I don't know. I guess you'll figure out what you're going to do next. Stay here or find somewhere else to head off to. Get a new job or an old one back. I don't know."

She let out a shaky breath. "You really think things will go back to the way they were with us? Have some big fight then just walk away and be back out of each other's lives again?"

"Yeah. I do."

Her eyes filled with tears. That couldn't happen. She wouldn't let it.

"I don't think I want to remember if that's the case."

He sighed. "I can't say I haven't had some of those same thoughts. But I can't honestly wish that on you, either. You deserve those memories, to be complete. The good and the bad. Those events, big or small make you who you are."

She wished she knew how to make him understand. She didn't want to lose him. She didn't want her angry, old self to come along and ruin whatever was happening to this new happier version.

"We had our reasons for splitting up, Chelsea. You had your reasons to feel the way that you did."

"Wrong reasons!"

"Maybe. But they were there, whether you remember right now or not. And you have a right to remember that and to feel that way. It isn't fair for you not to have the whole story to this, to not know your side of it all."

How could she explain that she was falling in love with him? She didn't want to remember what happened before if it meant going back to all that anger and sadness. The past didn't matter. All she knew was right now.

Ben went to stand. His car was packed and waiting. "I should head out. I have work in the morning."

"Ben…"

"Come here," he said, walking over and pulling her to her feet. Strong arms gathered her up, hugging her close. "I have missed you every single day. Hell, I miss you right now. And if I could go back, or make things different without question, I would."

Her head fell against his chest. "I don't want you to go."

"I know, baby." He kissed the crown of her head. "But I got to go. I'll be back in a couple of days or if you need me, I'll be here. You can call or text me whenever you want."

Chelsea nodded despite her tears. She followed behind him as he grabbed his coat, slipped it on, and reached for the door.

Ben spun around, reaching for her next. "Are you going to be alright?"

She wanted to beg him to stay, but instead she nodded her head.

Ben used his thumb to tilt her head back to look at him. There was a mix of emotions swirling in those dark eyes of his. Not giving him time to think better of it, she stood on her tiptoes and wrapped her arms around his neck, pulling him to her lips. His broad shoulders tensed beneath her fingertips. He sucked in one quick breath, then another before sliding his tongue against hers.

He tasted like mint and *Ben* and was so achingly familiar she kissed him again.

Ben gave her one hell of a long look once their lips parted. He pulled away, his hand squeezing hers. Neither of them spoke. What could be said? Chelsea stood in the doorway as he climbed inside his car. Saw the dust swirl behind his tires as he drove away. Then she watched it settle as though this had all been a dream.

Chapter Eight

Where Chelsea's house was warm and inviting, Ben's condo was the complete opposite. It wasn't just the stark black and white color scheme, it was everything that went along with it. The emptiness spoke volumes about the man he had become after their divorce.

His expensive new place didn't feel like home. It never had.

Anywhere without Chelsea never would.

Ben went to the kitchen and poured himself a drink before putting some of his stuff away. He left the rest of his things laid up against the corner of the door and went to take a long shower and change before heading to bed. He was dead on his feet and didn't need to show up at work looking like a zombie in the morning.

He definitely shouldn't be obsessing over a certain blonde back in Saltridge.

But that was exactly what he was going to do.

Chelsea was miserable.

The days since Ben's departure felt as though an entire month had been stuffed inside each one individually.

Several more memories came back to her, ranging from getting drunk at some bar, to temporarily working as a waitress in one of the few mom and pop restaurants around town, to even getting a glimpse of the first time she met Ben. That one she wished she could get more of, but her mind didn't respond to commands about such things.

There were other memories, too. Random things from school, teachers, strange faces she didn't recognize, names she couldn't quite recall. Most were short flashes, others were simply feelings, and a few were a total recall.

Memories of Ben were the hardest to deal with. There was one in particular that broke her heart. Ben looked so broken as he stood at the bottom of the stairs, making sure to keep a safe distance as she yelled at him. His eyes were filled with pain as he begged her to listen. But she wouldn't. Red hot fury ran through those stubborn veins of hers and she wouldn't have any of it. He tried several times to get a word in, but she always cut right in and tore back into him.

She also remembered Veronica's face. She didn't know why, but suddenly she could conjure up the image of the spite-filled blonde. Something inside her clicked as waves of anger and absolute despair shook her to the core.

Chelsea was jumping at every sound, and constantly getting up to see if Ben had arrived. She was so lost in thought, she nearly jumped out of her skin when a knock came at the door.

"Shit." She stole a glance at the clock then hurried over to the door, stepping quickly up to the peephole. "Ben…"

Somehow, he looked better today than he had just a few days ago. Her heart skipped a beat as she took him in and that same longing, she didn't logically understand roared its way back to life.

Ben sucked in a breath, his eyes looking her up and down. "Chelsea," he greeted. "You're looking better."

She smiled, thankful he noticed. "Thank you."

Chelsea let him in and felt her knees weaken when he passed by. "How have you been?" she asked, closing the door behind her.

She knew through their text messages what the high points of his days were, but it didn't compare to having him tell her in person.

"Good," he answered, looking around the front of the house. "Busy, but nothing too terrible. You get settled in? Had any trouble?"

Chelsea shook her head. "Things have been good. Maybe a little lonely and frustrating at times, but that's to be expected, I guess. Not much else has happened other than what I've already told you. I finally called to schedule my follow up appointment and got some more flowers from one of the shops around town, which was nice."

Ben asked more about her appointment and offered to take her. "Any new memories?"

Yeah! There's been quite a few of us naked and doing naughty things. Which I wouldn't mind recreating.

Chelsea was tempted, but instead she told him about a couple other things that had come back to her. She also kept the Veronica bit to herself, not wanting to waste any of their time together dwelling on that crazy woman.

Ben couldn't stay cooped up in this house. He missed her more than he expected and the temptation to reach over was just too fucking strong. His hands already lost the battle, lifting her smooth legs and draping them across his lap.

He could touch her leg. There was nothing wrong with that.

Her ankle was fine, completely safe.

The top of her thigh was just… right, there, too.

He cleared his throat. "We should go somewhere. Get you out of the house for a while."

"We could go to the beach. I didn't want to go alone." Chelsea glanced up from the magazine in her lap. "Or we could check out one of those indoor trampoline places."

His cock twitched at the memory. "Chelsea…"

"...Benjamin."

He sighed.

She smiled.

These new memories were fun. "Come on," he said. "We'll rock paper scissors on the way."

"Hey, Ben?"

"Yeah?"

Chelsea smiled. She was up to something. "You wouldn't happen to have some big fear of heights or speed or anything, right?"

"Why?"

"Good," Chelsea said. "Come on!" She tugged on his hand. The same hand that she hadn't let go of since the car. It was a habit, the way he casually laced their fingers over the center console. A slip. He noticed immediately, but there was something about the way she looked at him that made it impossible to pull away.

Ben gazed up at the mammoth metal structure. "Are you sure this is a good idea? You're recovering from a concussion."

"Which is exactly why we're not doing that," she said, pointing to the human catapult. "It's just go-karts. Now, come on!"

Ben had a genuine smile on his face, and Chelsea was laughing so hard that her stomach hurt. Why hadn't they gone through her photo albums before? Chelsea was sure more memories from the times in those books would be hitting her in days to come, but a few things were already fuzzy from just looking at the pictures. When they got to one of her and Ben covered in mud, a memory from one of their first dates struck. The night had gone tragically wrong, but in all of the right ways.

Chelsea liked the look on his face as they talked about that day and night. She liked it even more when he suddenly leaned forward, pressing his lips against hers.

"What was that for?"

He smiled again. "Nothing. Just good memories."

She returned his smile with one of her own. Before he could come to his senses or crawl back into his shell of indifference, she kissed him again, this time with more urgency. Ben's hands found their way to her, getting tangled up in her hair as he tugged her closer.

Chelsea moaned low in her throat.

Ben quickly pushed the photo albums out of the way and guided her leg over his so that she was straddling him. His hands came down to her hips. "Do you remember the rest of that night?"

"Yes."

And she did.

She remembered stealing Nate's truck when Ben's car ran into issues, the two of them getting lost along the way. The drive out to the beach after the mud war, jumping in the water and trying to get some of the sludge off of them, ending up in a position much like this in the back of Nate's old pickup. She remembered how it felt to be wrapped up in his arms just like this, their bodies entangled with one another.

She remembered how much she wanted him.

Ben let out a low chuckle. "I was aware of that. And of how much I thought I was going to pass out if I didn't get us both naked right there under the stars, but there wasn't any way I was going to let our first time be in that damn truck bed."

"I don't think I would have minded. We made the most of it that night, though."

He nodded against her, his fingertips sliding under the bottom of her shirt to touch her warm skin.

Chelsea closed her eyes, holding him closer to her as he began kissing up the side of her neck.

"I've missed you."

Chelsea wasn't sure if he meant just the past few days or in the past year and a half, but she didn't ask. Her hands toyed in his hair then ran down his shoulders and upper back until his lips returned to her. Her body moved against his, seeking more of him. Chelsea could feel his hardened length under her and it both thrilled and terrified her. She knew they had sex before, many, many times. Very amazing sex from the little she could recall. But for the most part, she was still the girl who had only ever been with one guy sexually, and only dated a handful of others before that.

Ben's blunt teeth nipped down her neck. His hands roamed her, obviously knowing exactly how to work her soft flesh. She arched into his touch as his fingers traveled down her spine, bucked her hips when he grabbed her breasts, and was begging him for more when his hands began rubbing up and down her inner thighs. Always close, but never touching exactly where she wanted him to.

"We shouldn't be doing this." His voice was husky.

"We're not in Nate's truck bed."

Ben sighed, pulling away from her. "No. Worse."

She sighed as well.

"I'm your ex-husband you don't really remember."

"I'm an adult, as are you," she countered. "A consenting adult."

"You wouldn't be if you could remember everything. Which makes this very, very wrong."

Chelsea let out a frustrated whine, placing both of her hands at the sides of his face. "The only thing I'm going to regret is watching you walk into that stupid guest room."

"Chels…"

Her head shook. "I want you."

Chelsea's words did the trick. Strong arms held tight as he took the steps two at a time. Her heart raced as he pulled her shirt over her head. Ben unsnapped her bra, letting the articles fall to the ground one by one.

"Lean back." She did as instructed, propping herself up on her elbows. Her eyes never left him as he sank down to his knees.

Chelsea swallowed as warm palms slid up her thighs. Ben hooked her legs over his shoulders and leaned his head down until his scorching lips circled her clit. She sucked in her breath as his tongue darted out, one foot twitching at the contact.

"Holy shit!"

One hand flew over her mouth while the other twisted through his dark locks. Her back arched so far her hips came off of the bed, but Ben held strong, which only turned her on more.

Chelsea wasn't sure if he was just skill, if it was chance, or if Ben just knew her body. Whatever the case, she was careening towards that blissful edge. He knew exactly where and how to touch her, at every given moment. It was beautiful torture.

Slowly, Ben lifted her legs off from where they were squeezing his head and folded them against her so her breasts were nearly touching. His hands held her just under her knees, but his mouth never seemed to leave her.

"Ben!" she moaned, bucking against him again, then trying to get loose. But he held firm, though it was more of a challenge in this position.

His fingers dug into her hips as his mouth clamped around her pulsating clit in one hell of a no-nonsense way. She screamed his name as he flicked his tongue. A burning sensation flooded her throat and reddish black spots took over her vision as he brought her over the edge.

The room was still spinning when Chelsea's eyes popped open. Ben was still poised between her thighs. "There's my girl."

Ben's mind was less muddled as he exited the restroom. More importantly, the throbbing in his balls was tempered. He took another deep breath. That wasn't supposed to happen. He tried preparing something to say when he was in the shower, but words were going to fail him right now.

It didn't matter. Chelsea's eyes did the talking. He couldn't do anything besides step deeper into her bedroom.

Chelsea's heart skipped a beat as she did a double take. "Who is that?" she asked, cutting into Amber's rambling, nudging her in the process.

"Who is who?"

"Tall, dark and far too gorgeous to exist," she answered, while casually attempting to point him out.

Amber rolled her eyes. "He's one of the guest speakers from Waterstone..."

Chelsea smiled as her dreams took her back to the very day she met Ben. But her smile morphed as sounds of an old argument flooded her. Not wanting to wake up, Chelsea tried to fight it, shutting the noise out, but then a door slammed, and she jumped to a near sitting position. It took but a second to realize she was alone in the room and another to realize she could hear Ben cursing up a storm outside.

Chelsea rushed downstairs and opened the door. Her eyes went wide as Ian Flint turned to face her there on the porch. "Chelsea," he greeted her with a charming smile.

Ben's hands were shaking as he paced back and forth. She didn't know what to say. Much less what was going on, but she was stuck watching as Ben stalked toward his car. "Ben?"

"Ben!" She shouted again as he climbed inside, but he paid no mind, driving off a few seconds later.

He looked pissed.

And now, she was terrified.

Chapter Nine

She could hear Ian talking, but he sounded muffled and far away.

"What the hell, Benjamin?"

He shot her one hell of a look, then turned to Ian.

"Get up," he growled out. "Both of you."

"Excuse me? We're having dinner, which is none of your concern."

He growled low in his throat. "Get. Up."

"Go to hell," Chelsea spat, her voice just above a whisper.

"Look, why don't you take a breath, calm down a little," Ian said, as he held his arms out in front of him, standing up from his chair. He didn't get a chance to say anything else as Ben's head tilted. He growled again and then the next thing anyone knew, he was on top of the blonde man, his fist connecting to Ian's face.

"Jesus fucking Christ, Ben!" Chelsea shouted, pulling him off. They had gathered the attention of every single person in the restaurant.

"Go outside," she ordered. "Now."

His eyes flashed.

She pointed at the door. "Go!"

Chelsea apologized to Ian, to the staff of the restaurant and everyone else who was there to witness what happened.

Ben spotted them once they were back outside and made a beeline for them.

"What the hell do you think you are doing?" she yelled before he got a chance to say anything else.

"Me?! What the fuck do you think you're doing?!"

"I am out on a date!"

He barked out an unamused laugh. His eyes grew wilder by the second.

"A date?" he repeated. "A date? In case you have forgotten, Chelsea Ann Black, you are my fucking wife."

This made her temper flare. "Excuse me?"

"I thought you said you were separated," Ian said.

Ben's head nearly snapped off as he looked at the banged up blonde man.

"Separated. Not divorced," he ground out. "As in, we are still motherfucking married."

"You really are something else, aren't you?" she said, stepping toward him.

"Don't you start," Ben warned, his murderous glare bouncing between her and Ian.

But she held her own. "You want to come in here, guns blazing, when we are legally separated? Yes, maybe we are still technically married-for now-but not for long. And even so, separation does stand for something, Benjamin. Unlike that shit you pulled."

"Chelsea. Don't start."

"You look good," Ian said.

Chelsea turned to look at him. She had no idea how long he had been standing there talking.

"What are you doing here, Ian?"

She certainly didn't reach out to him. "I, uh, I heard you were in a pretty bad accident," he said, looking down at his feet. "I was back in Saltridge for a couple of nights. I thought I would swing by and just see how you were."

Chelsea put a hand up to her head. "That's very sweet. It is. And I appreciate the concern, but I am doing better. Slow but steady progress."

He nodded and looked down the road for a minute. "You and him, huh?"

Chelsea sighed. What could she say?

He gave a tight smile. "You don't owe me or anyone else any kind of explanation. I just hope you know what you're doing."

"What?"

"I just meant things were pretty, um, intense with the two of you from the last I saw."

Chelsea closed her eyes. She very much wanted to be anywhere else right now. "Look, Ian about-"

He held up his hands. "Hey! No harm. No foul. Remember? As long as you're happy."

Sighing again, Chelsea gently said that he should probably leave.

"You know, I was thinking the same thing."

Chelsea was on the phone with Danielle when the line beeped. It was Ben. “I’ll call you back!” She didn’t even wait for a response before switching the call over. Her fingers shook as she held the phone back to her ear. “Ben?”

He sighed. “Yeah.”

“Thank God. I’ve been so worried. I’m so sorry. I don’t know why Ian showed up here. We haven’t spoken. I swear.” Her words overlapped, rushing out of her one after the next.

Ben was quiet for a moment. Then, she heard him suck in a breath and tell her it was okay but that he needed to get out of there. One reason being he thought he would go after Ian again. But the other reason he described had her trembling even more.

"Ben? Where are you?"

She heard what sounded like a glass being put down. "The bar."

"Are you drunk?"

That was the last thing any of them needed.

"No," he said. "I’ve had a few drinks, but I'm not drunk."

Another buzz rushed through her. "Would you come back to the house, then? Please?"

He gave a low chuckle. "That’s probably not the best idea, Chels."

"Yeah? Why not?”

“I can still taste you on my tongue.” Ben’s voice dropped several octaves. “Hear those delectable noises you always make when my face is buried between your thighs. I can still feel your legs shuddering against me… You *never* belonged to Ian."

Chelsea leapt from the sofa. Someone was at the door. Nearly an hour had passed since Ben hung up the phone.

A chill ran through her when their eyes met. She could almost hear his thoughts.

"Ben."

"You need to tell me to leave." His voice was dripping with need. He wanted her. Long fingers gripped the frame of the door as he openly gaped. "You need to tell me to leave," he repeated. "Please. I'm trying to do the right thing here."

Chelsea stepped back.

He knew it was an invitation.

And she knew what would come of it.

Ben's hard body pressed her against the cool metal, slamming the door closed. His lips demanded access and Chelsea moaned once his tongue finally slid against her own, then shivered as his hand slipped into the waistband of her pajama bottoms.

"Yes," she hissed as two digits slid inside her.

"Fuck." Chelsea moaned again, her head falling back, legs parting.

Her cotton shorts and silky thong were gone with a growl. Ben almost looked dangerous as he sank to his knees. Broad shoulders forced her thighs apart as he positioned his mouth against her glistening center.

Chelsea's hands flew down, grabbing at his hair and neck. She screamed out his name as his tongue formed a hard line and licked her slit before finding its way inside her aching core.

Ben's mouth moved slow and steady. His tongue darted in and out, tracing circles, kissing and teasing her swollen lips. Warm breath rolled over her clit and her back arched as her hips rocked.

His dark gaze held strong as he leaned closer. Hot lips circled her neglected bundle of nerves just as his tongue dashed a series of hard flicks. Chelsea's eyes snapped shut, and the door rattled as her head slammed back. "Yes…" she hissed. "Just. Like. That."

Ben groaned as thick fingers rejoined his talented tongue. Her thighs trembled. "Ben?"

Another groan. "Hmm?"

"I think I'm going to… Oh-God," she gasped. "I… am."

Ben's fingertips dug deeply into her thigh as she twisted and tugged on his dark roots. Sparks of pleasure rolled into waves of unfiltered bliss. Sound disappeared. The foyer erupted into a sea of brightly colored stars. Chelsea's back arched off the cool metal, toes curling, fingernails digging into Ben's neck. Her breath hitched and lungs burned as noises she didn't recognize tore from her lips.

Ben growled, rolling back and lowering them to the ground. Fingertips pressed hard into her thighs as he pulled her down to sit on his face.

Sparks were still dancing in her peripheral when Chelsea fell forward, swatting at his head. "Not again…"

"Such a good girl," Ben said, licking at her one last, very long time, which made her whole body twitch. He slid out from under her, his hands never leaving her skin. His touch was light as a feather as he grazed the back of her thighs, danced over her buttocks, and up her back.

Chelsea turned over and helped slip her tank top off. He didn't bother hiding his appreciative gaze. "You are the most beautiful woman I have ever seen, Chelsea Sanders. I cannot stand the idea of anyone else touching you. I don't want anyone touching you but me."

"Black," Chelsea said, shaking her head. "Chelsea Black… And I don't want anyone else."

Ben's voice cracked. "I need you."

Ben ground his teeth together. This was going to be over before it started. He had been on edge ever since she opened the door. Then there was the sweet torture of watching her come undone at his hand.

And now the damn woman was insistent on touching him.

Ben had a fingernail digging into each of his palms. It was like their first time together all over again. Chelsea's curiosity damn near mirroring memories she lost. Her wide eyes were filled with wonder. He bit back another moan as her fingertips danced back up his shaft. She lightly grabbed him, swirling her palm all the way down his base. His legs shook when she repeated the motion, and his eyes rolled back once she went in again.

Chelsea's perfect pout smiled in triumph as the first bead of moisture rolled down his mushroom tip. Soft fingers gathered the liquid, massaging it into his rigid flesh. She glided over every vein, ridge, and curve collecting the fluid until he couldn't fucking take it, thrusting wildly into her palm.

Ben bit into the foil packet, tearing it open. Chelsea didn't blink as the latex rolled into place and her fingers threaded through his hair as her supple thighs wrapped around him. Ben lowered down, kissing her hungrily.

It was her hand that reached between them.

"Chels…" Ben's head shook against her neck and his eyes stung as Chelsea's grip on his hair tightened. "Are you-"

His words morphed into a long moan as Chelsea shuddered around him. Her silky walls fluttered at the intrusion and clamped down when he inched further. "Fuck," he hissed as warm heat sealed around him.

Ben forced every single one of his corded muscles to lock. Chelsea could handle him. But he needed a damn minute.

Chelsea clawed down his shoulders once more, her hips shifting with need. Ben slowly pulled away, before plunging back, eliciting some of his favorite sounds.

A chant.

A plea.

A promise.

Ben grabbed her wrists and pinned them down to the bed just above her head. Her legs rose higher, giving him deeper access. Chelsea's head dug back into the pillow as his pace increased, moaning his name over and over.

"Do you know what you do to me?" There were no words to explain how much he missed this, missed her. It went well beyond sex, but it was part of the package. She was his home, where he needed to be.

Ben fell into a frantic pace as the day caught back up with him.

Their happy past, their bad one. All the fighting, the anger.

Ian.

Missing her.

Wanting her.

Chelsea's toes curled against the wall just above her head. She screamed nearly loud enough to shake the entire house, kicking her twisted leg when he reached for her sensitive clit and gave it a hard flick.

Ben fell into an unsteady pattern as her warm wet walls convulsed around him. "You were made for me. You're mine," he growled, slamming into her one last time.

Chapter Ten

Chelsea's staring woke him up. Ben blinked a couple of times as memories from just a couple of hours ago came rushing back. "Hey," he said softly, his voice still groggy from sleep.

"You okay?"

Chelsea nodded.

"You sure?" he asked before yawning. "What's on your mind?"

Her head shook. "It's stupid. And nothing. Really."

Ben yawned again. Reaching over to the lamp beside the bed, he switched it on. The two of them were still naked, barely covered under her pale-yellow sheets. He could make out the shape of her body underneath the thin cotton and felt a stirring of need as his eyes lingered a little too long. "What is it? You can tell me."

Chelsea was quiet for a moment, then sighed, looking away. "I don't know. I was just wondering about earlier, I guess. Was last night? Just because of Ian showing up? Trying to prove a point or something?"

Ben's head tilted to the side. "No," he said. "I wanted you, Chelsea. I have always wanted you. Did I get upset about suddenly seeing Flint at the door? Absolutely. But it went well beyond that."

"You sure?"

"Yes, I am. I've been failing to keep my emotions in check around you for a while now. We're in one hell of a complicated situation, and I've been trying to do the right thing by not mucking things up any further. I wanted to be there for you. Help you get things sorted and just wait for the other shoe to drop, I guess. But it wasn't as simple as that once I was there."

Chelsea smoothed a hand down his chest and scooted closer.

Ben sighed, letting his head fall back against the headboard. "It's not an easy place to be. I fell in love with you over five years ago. Despite all the fighting and the shit that went down between us, that hasn't changed. I have loved you every single day since I met you and missed you every day you've been gone. But I was doing my best to accept things. To get on with life. When I got the call that you were in an accident, it felt like the world was sinking beneath my feet. There wasn't much that I could do, and so I sat there wishing for a way to go back and change things between us."

Chelsea slowly looked up from her hand.

"I was all over the place those days you were unconscious. One second, I was panicking over the worst-case scenario. Next, I would sit there and plan out some elaborate speech, praying something would get through to you. Eventually, I always circled back around the most likely case. That you would wake up and all hell would break loose. You would erect that wall back around you, forcing me to take off with my tail between my legs."

"But then I woke up, and I didn't remember any of it?"

Ben nodded. "I wasn't prepared for that. Thank God you were asleep. I didn't know what I was supposed to do. After a while, when you woke up, I just shut down. I forced myself to calm down and bite everything else back, put myself in neutral to test the waters."

Ben paused for a moment, looking her over. "I was expecting life to just go back to normal. You to send me packing. But then, you didn't remember anything. Not me. Not us being together or falling apart, the good or the bad. Which was a fucking disaster waiting to happen."

"How so?" Chelsea asked.

"You woke up with amnesia and honestly, not in the best shape otherwise. You were states away from home, from any of your friends, and you had all this shit dumped on you. There was no way in hell I was going to leave you there like that. Alone. I wanted to make sure you were being taken care of, and honestly, as someone who knew you best, I was seen as the best bet on getting your memory back. Thankfully, I was in a position with work where I could take as much time off as I needed to get a handle on everything. But it's not easy to be around you. To rehash the past that you don't remember, meanwhile I do. To keep waiting for shit to hit the fan once you finally do have all those memories back."

She looked down again. "I know that none of this is fair to you."

"So much of me wishes it was as simple as saying fuck the past, we're here right now. But that's not fair to you. You deserve your memories. You deserve all those pieces coming back into place. And I want you to have them. I just… I want you to want me still when you have them back, too. But I have no control over that. It's an endless tug-of-war. I want to spend time with you. To be here. I want to hold your hand, kiss you, touch you, and sleep next to you. I want to say fuck everything else most of the time and just get lost in you, have everything that I want back again for a while and deal with the consequences later. Friday night, I got swept up in everything and I didn't want to fight it. I swore I wouldn't let it go further than that afterward, but then I wake up and Ian's banging on the damn door. And I just-"

"I didn't know he was going to be here," Chelsea said softly.

"I know. But he was here, and I needed to leave before history played itself out again. I was angry and jealous. I was mad over the fact that we ended, remembering the last time you shacked up in here with Ian, and how that led to dissolving the remaining fragments of our relationship. I was mad about everything. About Veronica and her bullshit, us splitting up, you being with someone else, just everything."

"Why did you come back?"

"You asked me to. And I wanted to. I wanted you, and I was tired of doing the right thing. I've been on an emotional roller coaster and I just needed you. I was jealous, I can't deny that. But it was so much more than that. It was a buildup of all the time you've been gone and how much I've missed you. It was me being in love with you and wanting to act on that, to show you. I don't know."

"Do you regret it?"

Ben shook his head. "I probably should. Last night wouldn't have happened if Ian hadn't shown up and become that final shove, and I should be more upset with myself for taking advantage of you since you didn't know our full history, but I don't regret doing it. This is exactly where I have wanted to be. Making love to you is all I have been able to think about since that first night in your apartment. And selfishly, I couldn't be happier. What about you? Any regrets?"

Chelsea quickly shook her head. "This is exactly what I have wanted since laying eyes on you, and that has only grown the more I know you, and as the memories slowly come back. So, no. I just wish it wasn't so complicated."

"I know."

The two fell quiet while Chelsea scooted closer.

"Ben?"

"Hmm?"

"This is going to sound crazy but are your feelings just for, you know, me with the memory and the past we had?"

Ben cut her off, leaning down to kiss her gently. "There's no you or her type of situation for me. I understand for you it must seem that way, but that's not how it is. You're just you. Memory or not. You're the same girl who played a battle of wits with me in front of a packed classroom. Who wanted to have picnics in all the different cemeteries around town. That tried showing off her French skills after meeting my cousin Jack's new wife and wound up calling her some dirty name by accident. You're still the girl I fell in love with, the bride who stood before everyone we knew and loved and who I promised forever to. The wife who gave me the best years of my life. There's no past or present, Chelsea, just you."

Chelsea let out a happy yelping noise when Ben saw her, lifted her up and sat her on the island counter. "Don't you have some food to be making me?" she asked, wrapping her arms around his neck.

"Just warming things up," he said with a wink. Then nodded to where the oven was preheating, and the pizzas were laid out.

"Uh huh."

"Mmhmm," he replied against her neck.

Her head fell back as Ben suckled her skin into his mouth, his hands sliding from her knees until they were under the shirt. She arched into him as his warm hands cupped her breasts. Then squeezed her thighs together when he twisted her hardened tips between his talented fingers.

They still hadn't figured out where to go from here, but she certainly didn't have any complaints about what he was doing to her now.

Chelsea groaned when he pulled away, watching as he went and put the frozen pizzas in the oven. He fiddled with his phone to set the timer before coming back over to her.

"You have to leave in a couple of hours, don't you?" she asked, pulling him closer.

He nodded. "Have a presentation to get to in the morning. My boss and a few others are flying in from the East Coast. Danielle's supposed to be coming down for the weekend, though, isn't she?"

Chelsea nodded. "Yeah, she said they'd be here around noon or so."

"At least you won't be alone," he offered, his hands sliding under the shirt and rubbing her back.

"Yeah, it should be fun. We have a few things mapped out to go do, and it feels like it's been forever since the last time I saw her and Penny. Wish you could stay, though. Which I am sure you will now offer to do or something, but at some point, you do have to work at a regular rate."

He chuckled, kissing at her temple. "This is true. I would say I'd come back, but I don't want to intrude on your girl time, either. I'll be back in a few days, though."

Which felt like a fucking eternity.

"You know, you look sexy as hell in my shirt," Ben said before taking her lips with his own.

"I think you pull it off better."

Ben shook his head, kissing down her neck. "Not even possible."

Chelsea blushed, holding on to him a little tighter when he moved her and came to stand between her legs.

“Can I ask you something?"

"Mmhmm."

Ben pulled back to look at her. "Do you still think I only slept with you because Flint was here?"

She was silent for a moment, then shrugged. "Not really, but I worried that it could have been possible. You're just so unreadable most of the time and I’ve only seen this shell of yours crack a few times, so I didn’t know. Then, I remembered what I did after we split and all of that craziness. I guess it was just weighing on me."

His eyes narrowed. "You remembered about Ian?"

Chelsea nodded. "Yeah. Some. Using him. The few dates we went on, that last where you showed up, guns blazing. Lots of anger and yelling, Ian getting punched in the face, coming back here."

Ben set his jaw at that. "You remember us fighting back here?"

Chelsea looked away as she nodded again. The words he flung at her still stung even now, and she felt sick at the ones she said.

Ben sighed, gathering her up in his arms. "I'm sorry," he whispered. "I'm sorry that night ever happened, and I said what I did. I told you before, I didn't mean it. Any of it. I get a little hot-headed sometimes and was fuming over you being with him. I lashed out like some bratty seven-year-old and have hated myself ever since."

"I wasn't exactly handling the situation any better than you. I put us in that mess."

Ben tilted her chin up and looked her in the eyes. "I am sorry. I didn't mean a word of it."

She tried to smile. "I know. I didn't either. Some of it was ringing true at that moment, but that would change."

Ben was never the best with words. He had no issue telling Chelsea he loved her, how beautiful she was, or the things he wanted to do to her, but he was always pretty straightforward. He relied more on actions to express himself and his feelings.

He was much better at that.

And he wasn't going to leave Chelsea with any doubts about how he felt.

Chelsea's hands spread out against the granite, fingers holding tightly to the edge as his own hands rubbed up and down her bare legs. She shivered each time his fingers brushed against her thighs, creeping further under the hem of her long shirt.

Ben bypassed the lacy material of her thong and groaned. She was already dripping wet and ready for him. His thumb parted her slippery seam, dipping into her warm channel before sliding up and circling her clit.

"Shit," Chelsea moaned, her hips moving against his hand. "That feels so good."

Her hair was tousled, lips swollen, eyes clouded with lust. Lindsey was right, he never stood a chance. He was so fucking gone, he would have sold her his damn soul if she even hinted at wanting him to. Ben tugged the flimsy underwear down her hips. "I need to be inside you."

Chelsea's face flushed at his confession, but she grabbed the back of his neck and pulled him to her, kissing him hard. His hands went to her hips, helping to angle her a bit better as he slipped on the condom he brought from upstairs.

"Fuck," Ben ground out, sliding into her silky heat.

"You look so good taking my cock." Chelsea's fingernails were marking half-moons into his shoulder blades, her legs squeezing him with all their might.

He couldn't get enough.

Ben pulled his shirt off of her after switching their positions, her body now straddling his. As Chelsea lowered down, she was pretty sure she could see stars, but something about being in this position made her feel uneasy. The way Ben was stretching her was nothing short of delicious, but she worried. Most of their intimate moments were fuzzy.

Chelsea's hands pressed into his chest as she leaned forward. "I don't know what I'm doing."

Ben's large hands gripped her hips. "Relax," he whispered, guiding her up, and back down his rigid flesh. "I've got you." His smooth voice encouraged her as much as his hands.

Ben groaned as she rotated her hips. "See," he said. "Nothing to worry about."

Ben's talented fingers teased her hard nipples, cupping her soft mounds in his palms, squeezing lightly. Her entire body shivered as his thumb brushed against her aching clit, completely wrecking her little stride.

"Ben," she said, her body shaking. "I need… something."

Ben smirked, lifting her up a moment later. He slowly thrusted into her as he carried her until her back was pressing into the far wall of the kitchen. Then, he bent down and took one of her nipples into his mouth. "You're so beautiful, you know that?"

Chelsea's eyes rolled back as his pace increased and one of his hands snaked down to tease her clit. Ben's other arm was doing its best to keep her still. His fingertips spread wide as they dug into her crossed wrists. Which led her to the conclusion that she must have a thing for being held down.

A kink Ben was obviously well aware of.

Her bottom and back smacked against the wall with every hard thrust, and soon Chelsea found herself biting her bottom lip as uncontrollable spasms took over.

Ben's fingers gave her throbbing clit one last pinch. She screamed out his name, her legs shaking so much she couldn't even feel them anymore. Ben laughed as they turned into jelly, but only for a moment. His fingertips dug into her skin as he fell into an unsteady rhythm.

Furiously, he kept thrusting until all the tension inside him snapped. Ben collapsed against her, chest heaving. "Atta girl."

Unable to hold them up any longer, Ben slipped to the ground. His breath was coming out in harsh pants, and he could still feel Chelsea trembling.

When his phone went off, signaling that he better get a move on, he nearly tossed the damn thing through the window. He didn't want to move, let alone leave her here again for the next few days. Not after this. He went half-crazy the last time. Not to mention all the hours he wasted due to Ian-fucking-Flint.

Ben took his sweet time picking himself up off her floor, kissing her, then going to gather his things.

"You know I'll stay if you want me to," he said when he spotted her standing in the doorframe.

Chelsea smiled. "I know," she said. "But we already discussed that. As much as I want you here, life has to go on. It will suck, but maybe it won't be so bad with Danielle here this time."

"Maybe not for you," he said, smirking her way.

"Can you call me when you get back?" she asked as she crawled onto the bed. She swiped his bag and took its place, wrapping her arms around his neck.

"Yeah, I can do that," he said, kissing the top of her hair. He nearly lost it when she lifted her head, and there were tears in her eyes. "Hey now, none of that."

"I'm sorry. I just hate when you're gone."

Ben leaned down to kiss her. "I hate it, too, baby."

He took a deep breath.

"I love you."

This only made her tears fall harder. "I love you, too."

Ben closed his eyes, his heart bursting with happiness while simultaneously ripping into pieces. As much as he dreaded walking out that door, nothing was going to compare to the hell he would face once Chelsea was whole again.

Chapter Eleven

Chelsea had just finished changing when Danielle and Penny knocked on her door. She smiled as she took the stairs down and helped the couple inside, fiercely hugging each of them.

"How are you settling in?" Danielle asked once she got her bags inside.

Chelsea smiled as she led the pair into the kitchen. "I'm doing okay. It's still weird being here and trying to put all the missing pieces together, but things are getting better every day. Accepting that those memories will come back as they please helped to calm me down. No use in stressing over something you have no control over."

"It seems like you have made a lot of progress, though," Penny said, climbing onto one of the bar stools.

"Yes and no." Chelsea shrugged. "I think being back in Saltridge has helped. It's just different and sometimes frustrating. But I'm doing my best. It does get lonely, though."

This made Danielle frown. "I know, and we all feel horrible about that."

"It's been an adjustment. In my head I feel and see things one way, so sometimes I have to catch myself. But Ben's usually here. I don't want to live off him forever, though, so I keep thinking I need to get in gear and maybe try to find something else to do while I'm putting my life back together. I just haven't quite gotten around to the actual 'doing' part yet."

"That could be a great idea," Penny said.

Danielle nodded. "Absolutely! When you're ready, that is."

Chelsea confided plenty to both Penny and Danielle about Ben, but she hadn't had the chance to fill either of them in on the last few days, so she slowly eased into bringing him up.

"I can say that I am both surprised and… not," Danielle said after a moment.

Penny raised her hand. "Seconding that."

"I know things are very, very complicated, and this is far from ideal timing, but I don't know. It feels right. I wish I knew how to explain it."

The two women listened as she tried, then the redhead took Chelsea's hand. "I just don't want to see you get hurt or watch the two of you repeat any of the past. I am glad that he's been here to help you out so much. And that he's finally had a chance to clear the air about what happened between you, but once the rest of your memories come back, you might not feel the same way. Veronica wasn't your only problem."

Chelsea sighed. "I know."

"I just don't want to see you hurt. Things got really ugly between the two of you and no one wants to see something like that happen again. But I will say this. You two were so in love before it all went to pieces like it did. If you two could work things out, if that is what you want, I support you one hundred percent."

"Really?" Chelsea asked, tilting her head to the side.

"Absolutely. You two would have a lot to work through, but you made each other happy once. Quite honestly, I don't think either of you have been complete since you split. Just make sure you don't get too deep into anything before you know what you truly want to do, okay?"

"God, I miss this place," Danielle said, her eyes closed and arms out wide.

"I can't believe I haven't made it out this way yet," Chelsea said, running her toes through the sand.

"So many good memories here," Danielle continued. "Good times with good friends."

Chelsea smiled. This place held a lot of their souls.

The beach was mostly deserted. There was a group of teenagers down by the rocks, and a guy walking his dog on the other side, but that was it. The skies were clear. It really was the perfect escape.

"We need to come out here more often this summer. Get Nate and Holly down here, too," Danielle said, taking a seat. "Feels like it's been forever since we've done that. We're always meeting up somewhere else with everyone scattered around."

Penny nodded, sitting beside Danielle and taking her hand.

Chelsea laid down, watching them, and watching the waves roll onto the bank. For the first time since arriving back in Saltridge, she could breathe again.

When they got back to the car, Chelsea checked her phone while the girls discussed what they might do with the rest of their time together. They threw around different ideas and Danielle was getting ready to pull out of their parking space when a black truck came out of nowhere and had her slamming on the brakes. "Shit," the redhead swore. "Is everyone okay?"

Chelsea's hands were shaking, but she was more angry than anything as she glared at the truck full of rowdy teenagers. But then Penny joked about what the wind had done to Danny's hair, and everyone cracked up.

They pulled up behind the truck, waiting to turn back out onto the main road, when they all heard an argument growing louder from the vehicle in front of them.

They watched in horror as it pulled out right in front of a large white van. The person driving the van didn't even have time to react before its front end collided into the passenger door.

Chelsea's eyes widened before she slammed them back shut, her hands reaching out for the headrest and holding on to it for dear life. She forced herself to breathe, but her chest protested something fierce, burning and stinging each time she inhaled.

"Oh my God!" Danielle shouted, jumping out of the car.

Penny stayed with Chelsea. "Are you okay?"

But Chelsea couldn't answer, just strangled out the breaths that were now coming in faster than she could handle.

Penny rubbed her cold hands. "Here, maybe getting you back out in the fresh air and sunshine will help."

Chelsea slipped down to the ground as soon as the door opened, her hands covering her mouth.

It took Penny a few more moments, but then it hit her. "Chelsea?" she said softly, rubbing the other blonde's back. "Are you-"

"Is she okay?" Danielle asked, running over to them out of breath.

"Um, I'm not sure."

Chelsea felt like she was dying. She couldn't hear anything, and her vision was blurry and dark.

That's when it hit her.

Those awful noises from the impact.

One image after the next. A thought, a feeling… love, pain… Ben… Veronica…. There were no breaks. Just a constant barrage of memories.

There was a large truck heading straight for her. Chelsea screamed as she began sliding on the icy road and soon hit yet another truck.

The impact knocked her out, but for a few short moments, she woke back up. A police officer was trying to talk to her as she blinked her eyes a few times. Her head hurt, her face hurt, everything hurt. She wanted to cry, or really, she wanted to pass right back out.

Her car was now upside down and that fact was not making anything better. She tried to speak but soon it was all black again.

There was a knock on the door. "Yes?" she called.

"What are you doing?"

Chelsea sunk down into the bubbly water. "Taking a bath."

"Mmm," Ben said. "Can I come join?"

Chelsea felt her face flush. "I-in the bath?"

"Yes."

She was silent for a minute. Then she got up and unlocked the door, hurrying back to sink in the bubbles as he came in.

"Hi there," she said shyly.

"Hello to you," he drawled, looking her over. His shirt came off just a few moments later, followed by the rest of his clothing, and then he was sliding into the tub behind her. He laughed as he gathered her into his arms.

"Why are you being all shy?"

"I don't know. I just never had someone want to take a bath with me."

"Now, that I highly doubt," he told her. "Beautiful naked woman and all…"

"Who is that?"

Ben turned his head to look at her. "Who is who?"

Chelsea took a step closer to him, then slyly pointed to the busty blonde across the room who was burning holes into the two of them.

"Oh, that's Veronica Craft."

"That's the woman you've been working with? You're joking."

"Why are there photos of her on your phone?"

Ben's face scrunched up. "What?"

Chelsea stomped over and picked the black phone up off of his desk. A sultry photo of Veronica was on the screen.

Ben took the phone from her, then reached into his pocket and pulled out another.

"That's not even my goddamn phone. This is," he said and handed it to her.

"And this is your, what, dummy phone to talk to her in private on?"

"No. I have no interest in Veronica Craft. None. As I have explained to you over and over again. I have not done anything with her, nor do I want to. I don't know how or why the phone is in here, but I've never touched it."

"You're really okay with moving here?"

Ben smiled at her. "Absolutely."

"It's a bit of a drive for you to go back and forth to work."

He shrugged and kissed her forehead.

"You're worth it," he told her with a wink. "Besides, with the promotion, I'll be able to change my schedule to work from home more. We'll get it all figured out. This is your home, Chels."

"Our home," she corrected.

Ben never lost his temper with her, not once. They argued, but he always kept a level head. So, when he did snap, she jumped back at the new side of him.

Gone was the sad, pathetic man begging for her to listen and in his place stood one pissed off force of a man. He cut her off, his words slicing her to the core. His rage only grew alongside hers and they both went off the damn deep end as time went on. She spewed every vile thing she could think of his way, and he had no qualms returning the favor.

They ripped one another to shreds anytime they were around each other. Cursing one another out, saying the other was awful in bed, how worthless they thought the other was, using secrets they confided in one another as weapons to bring up and throw back in the others' face.

They had been trying to have a baby before shit hit the fan, and Ben pulled that out the night with Ian. He used every awful thought that popped into his head. He practically cackled when he brought up the baby they had only barely tried for, voicing what a bullet he dodged.

In return, she told him she wished he'd kill himself so she would be free of him for good.

She was screaming at him, words she'd said a million times over by this point. He tried to get in a word of his own, but she wouldn't let him.

Finally, when she told him to leave, he cursed at her, ran upstairs, and got a bag together.

She started crying, following him upstairs a few minutes later and stood in the doorway as he threw clothes into his gym bag.

"So, you're really going to go?"
"You're the one fucking telling me to leave, Chelsea! I'm done hearing you blame me for shit that I haven't done. You want me gone? Then I am fucking gone."

Chelsea didn't know why, but she just wanted him to look at her.

But he wouldn't. And it was eating her up inside.

Ben hadn't once in the hallway, in the courtroom, nor was he now after having followed her out.

Their divorce was officially granted. Finalized. It was done.

And he wouldn't even look at her.

Chelsea felt her insides twisting up as her gaze bore into his retreating backside.

His face had been stone-cold as had been for what felt like forever.

He didn't fight anymore, hadn't in a long time.
Now, he was walking away, possibly forever.

And not for the first time she regretted everything.

She could have stopped this. She could have told him the truth.

"I think I found a job," Chelsea said, taking a seat on Danielle's couch.

"That's great!" Danielle replied, taking the paper out of Chelsea's hands and looking it over. "Wait, what? Texas? You can't move to Texas."

Chelsea laughed. "Why not? It could be good for me."

"Because! Because it's too far away and you don't know anyone there—and it's too far away!"

Chelsea couldn't breathe. Couldn't think. Her fingers clutched her head as she fought the onslaught of unwelcomed images. All the rage. The hate. The anger.

After running as fast as she could, Chelsea got into the first cab she saw, which happened to already be carrying a passenger. The man looked scared for a second, but then just held up a hand and said to hell with it. So, she climbed in and let herself have a nice breakdown as they drove.

When they arrived at the bar, she got out of the cab and went straight for the bathroom where she had another breakdown, turned her phone off, and tried to fix herself up before going back into the dark bar. She ordered a drink and found a corner to wallow in., but the blonde stranger sought her out.

She tried politely shooing him away at first, but when he didn't take the hint, she got snippy. However, he laughed it off, sitting down with her despite her saucy attitude.

Somehow, she started spilling her guts to the British stranger, telling him all about how she caught her cheating husband. How she should have known better. Somehow, this also led to finding out that her stranger knew the stupid bimbo. Mitchell Craft was his name, and she, of course, asked if there was a connection, which there was.

Half-siblings.

That just made Chelsea fume more.

Mitch, as he told her, ripped into his dear sister nearly as badly as Chelsea had, which made her like him just a tad bit more. So, they drank, and they bitched about Veronica, and about Ben, and everything else under the sun.

The night was fuzzy, but she could remember him hinting more than once about taking her home. She brushed it off and when she had her fill of the seedy bar, she prepared to go somewhere. She wasn't sure where, yet. But she called a cab, bid her stranger farewell, and went outside to get some fresh air while she waited for her ride.

Then, arms were on her, roughly pulling her into an alleyway. Mitch was all over her, calling her "love" and telling her how beautiful she was. She pushed him away and screamed for him to let her go. But he refused, holding her tighter. He started going on about how they would make Ben pay for fucking around with Veronica, and that he could be a sweet revenge. She still refused, fighting, kicking, screaming at him. But then he head butted her, practically knocking her out.

When she came to, she was in a strange bed, in a room she didn't recognize. She was alone which she was thankful for, but terrified by the fact she was naked.

Her body hurt.

Her heart hurt.

After getting dressed, she was about to leave when Mitch came in. She felt like throwing up as he stalked toward her. He put a finger to her lips, then threatened her with that same soft voice from back at the bar. He almost sounded sweet as he listed all the things he would do to her if she ever breathed a word about their night together.

Chelsea's entire body shook as she got into the elevator and pressed the button for the lobby. She couldn't deal with this. Not with everything else going on.

Chapter Twelve

Ben absentmindedly scratched his head as he glanced at his phone. He sighed again. He was overreacting. Chelsea had been silent now for several hours, but that didn't have to mean something was wrong. She was probably just catching up with Danielle and Penny or taking a nap or something. It wasn't the end of the world.

Yet, he worried anyway.

He missed her like crazy.

When they separated, it was like he had to go through withdrawals. Which was nearly what he felt now. He got just a taste of that back with the accident and now here he was, missing her all over again.

Ben pushed his phone off to the side. A shower would pass some time. Then, all he had to do was make it through work tomorrow and he could head back to Saltridge.

He was just reaching his bedroom when someone knocked at the door.

Ben's eyes widened as he opened the door. "Chelsea," he greeted. "What are you doing here?" he asked, stepping out of the way to let her in.

Chelsea had never been to Ben's new apartment, but the look of it didn't surprise her. It was large and luxurious. She bet he paid a pretty penny for it, too. Everything was neat and in order, black and white hues taking over the majority of the space. It was just as his office had been, both at home and in the building of Waterstone. On his own, he was pretty predictable with these kinds of things.

Chelsea wasn't sure what it was she did or said, but it didn't take long for Ben to realize that she regained her lost memories. A fresh wave of emotions passed over his handsome face. Confusion, guilt, sadness—all of them finally settling into his familiar mask of neutrality.

She felt a sharp pain in her chest as she watched him shut down in a matter of seconds. She could practically read his thoughts.

It was heartbreaking.

"Are you okay?" Ben asked after a few more seconds.

His tone was as emotionless as his face.

She nodded.

"Do you want something to drink? Want to sit?"

Chelsea cleared her throat. "A glass of water would be fine, thank you." She looked around Ben's space some more while he was in the kitchen. It didn't escape her that the last time she was around him he was telling her that he still loved her, and the last time she was fully herself around him, another world war nearly broke out.

Both things made her equally nervous.

She watched as Ben carefully handed her glass to her, then stepped several feet back, leaving ample space between them. He wasn't going to break the bubble of awkwardness they were under. He wasn't going to be the one to bring them into the present.

She let out a long sigh as she glanced around the apartment once more. "There was an accident back in Saltridge," she said quietly. "This group of teenagers was being careless and caused an accident while Penny, Danielle, and I were heading back to my house after spending some time out at the beach."

"Was everyone okay?" he asked. "Are you okay?"

Chelsea nodded, taking a sip of her water. "We weren't involved. I think everyone is going to be fine. They took everyone to the hospital, and I've been trying to keep up with any news here and there."

Ben nodded. "That's good."

Chelsea felt her hands wanting to shake, so she walked over to put her glass down on his coffee table. Several moments passed before she took a deep breath. "I was coming to see you," she told him. "When the accident happened—my accident. I was coming to see you."

This got his attention. "What?"

Another deep breath. "I was coming back here to see you," she repeated. "Well, that had been the plan, at first. With how crazy the weather and the roads were, I began to think twice about it. I was going to pull over for the night. Maybe let the roads clear up, figure out what I was even going to do or say. I could see the exit sign and was ready to pull off the road for the night, but then everything else happened."

His eyes narrowed after a moment. "Why? Why were you coming to see me?"

Danielle hadn't exactly been wrong when she mentioned having doubts about what happened between Ben and Veronica.

She was questioning what the truth was.

"I asked you to leave me alone and when I got exactly that, I missed you," she said. "Everything had been so go, go, go. There was rarely time for me to sit back and figure out my feelings or sort through what was happening. Then, all I had was time to think. And to realize how big of a mess everything was."

With a small smile, she also added that most of those questions she came to ask him, she already got the answers to.

Just not how she intended.

But, like with everything else, there was more to it.

She was so angry for so long and took it out on Ben, whether he was around to hear it or not. It was good to get away and be on her own. It scared her relentlessly to be by herself, to be so far from everyone she had known, but it made her stronger in some ways. She never told a single soul what had happened that night with Mitch, and it had been eating away at her every minute since.

Some days were worse than others, but it was always there. The rape made her afraid in ways she had never been before. She felt so weak. Dirty and ashamed. Guilty and then even angrier because she knew better than to allow such thoughts.

The rage nearly consumed her. She had been so angry at herself. For feeling ashamed, for taking it out on everyone.

Angry for blaming Ben, for keeping it to herself. Pissed it ever happened in the first place. She hated herself for not believing Ben. For running out like she did, for getting into the cab, for drinking that night, for not taking more precautions.

She hated herself more after Ben kept declaring his innocence regarding Veronica. In some twisted way, what happened with Mitch made her feel as though she had betrayed him, and that disgusted her. How could she explain that?

Something snapped inside her after that fateful night.

Anytime she saw Ben, she immediately went into attack mode because, in her head, he was to blame for everything. It was on the tip of her tongue more than once to flat out accuse him for what Mitch did. She said many truly awful things to him, but she never crossed that line. Which she was beyond grateful for. It wouldn't have just broken him. If she said those words out loud, it would have killed her, too.

Instead, she let all the rage seep into every aspect of her life.

She wanted him to hurt because she was. She continued to accuse him of cheating because she would rather fight and argue than give him an inch and have to explain what was really wrong. Which only pissed her off more because she was having to ruin something beautiful.

All because a nightmare had become her reality, and she didn't want him to know.

It was easier to fight than to feel.

But when he shut down on her, it hurt worse than any of the arguments had.

He gave up.

The broken man, the angry one—she could handle that, but the one who didn't react anymore? That didn't care? That cut deep. By the end, it wasn't as if she could blame him for being tired of fighting or giving up on her.

After all, it was what she wanted.

It was why she began acting this way, so that he would leave her alone.

It wasn't until she moved out of state, and had the space to breathe, that everything sank in and she really processed what happened. She thought about all the things Ben said and ways he tried to prove that nothing happened between him and Veronica. How differently she could have handled things if she only told Ben what happened.

She looked around her new life and realized what a mess she had created.

She missed him.

She missed everything.

Chelsea swallowed hard as she took a seat on the leather couch and tried to answer him. She briefly touched on some of the earlier events with Veronica, as well as a couple of their more prominent issues. She took another quick drink before getting to the night she walked in on Veronica in his hotel room.

Ben stiffened at the first mention of that night, his hands clenching around his glass. She took a deep breath as she began walking him through those dreadful hours from her point of view. Slowly, she explained what happened to her after she went running from that room.

She told him about running down the hall, and pushing the button for the elevator. How she heard him yelling and took off for the closest staircase. About the guy, the driver, and how she didn't have any idea where to go, so she simply instructed him to take her to the closest place with alcohol. About the bar, how she hadn't paid any attention to where they were going, or where they were, until they came to a stop. She described the building, the big neon sign flashing above the door. How she turned her phone off before she even got out of the cab.

Chelsea picked at her nail polish as she described the seedy little bar, the pretty brunette bartender who was working that night, and how thankful she was that she simply poured the drinks and didn't ask questions. She made sure that Ben understood she was planning on finding a corner to disappear into, but that those plans got ruined by the guy from the cab.

She explained how once enough liquor was in her, she told the stranger about her night, about finding her husband with another woman. How she was cursing him, Veronica, and any other man who made the mistake of looking her way, and how that led into her finding out that this stranger she shared a cab with was related to the damn blonde.

She admitted that Mitch hit on her several times, and kept making crude jokes, but she brushed him off. Taking another drink from the cup before continuing, she went over the turning point of that night when suddenly Mitchell Craft was grabbing for her, pulling her into his arms.

"He said I should go home with him to teach you a lesson. That he would make me forget all about you," she said quietly. "His hands were still on me, holding me roughly. He tried to smile, but something wasn't right. He was too serious."

Chelsea told Ben every detail she could recall. Much of

what happened at that motel was fuzzy. There were a few blurry images that would come and go, which she tried to describe.

Ben walked over, making her jump. He took a seat on the coffee table in front of her, taking her hands into his. This simple act had tears forming in her eyes as she recounted waking up naked, her entire body battered and bruised. The blood on the sheets, how it wasn't much, but it was there.

Chelsea broke as she tried to explain where things went from there, but Ben hurried to pull her tightly in his arms.

"Shh," he whispered, rubbing her back. "Chelsea," he said after several minutes passed. "You should have told me. I could have helped you, done something."

This only made the tears flow harder. "I didn't want you to think of me as—"

He shook his head. "I wouldn't have thought that, Chels. Never. I wouldn't have thought any less of you and it kills me you think I would have."

"I didn't really," she whispered. "It was just, it was all in my head. Nothing made sense. I didn't want you to think less of me because of it. I didn't even want to acknowledge that it happened, I didn't want to deal with it. I just-"

Ben's strong arms wrapped around her, pulling her into his lap. "Stop. It's okay. I'm here. I'm here, and I've got you."

"Did she know?" Ben asked. "Did Veronica know?"
He was now up and pacing the floor.
Chelsea toyed with her fingers again. "I don't know."

"You need to make a police report."

"What? I couldn't do that. It was two years ago."

"So? It still happened, and you can still report it."

"And what good would that do now?"

Ben gave her an angry look before quickly softening his features. "Because it will help you," he said, walking over to her. "Because if she or anyone else was involved in what happened to you, they should pay for that."

Ben let out a deep breath. Of all the scenarios he imagined, he never expected this. He rubbed at his temples as he fought to find the best way to tell her that Mitchell Craft died in a skiing accident some months ago. He couldn't recall much about it but had seen the obituary on one of his socials.

"Honestly? I think that makes me feel better. Strange as it sounds. At least I don't have to worry about him doing the same thing to some other poor girl."

Ben's eyes narrowed. "I would have broken his neck."

"I know."

She had been there. She thought about making a report so many times. There were many nights she lay awake, berating herself, worried that he was out there doing the same thing to someone else and how that would be her fault.

Chelsea shook her head, reaching out to cup his face. "Ben, honestly, all I want to do is put this behind me. And for the first time, I feel like that might actually be possible. I've been living under the weight of everything for so long, and I just want to get past this and worry about the future instead."

His head tilted to the side as he closed his eyes. "How am I supposed to do that? This was my fault. I should have listened to you. I should have been faster in chasing after you that night. Hell, I shouldn't have even gone on the damn trip. I should have protected you. That was my job."

Chelsea leaned down to kiss him. "It was his doing, Ben. At the end of the day, whether someone else was involved in planning it or not, it was his doing. No matter what was going on, it boiled down to him and him alone. I spent a lot of time and energy blaming you, and it wasn't right to do that."

Ben shook his head. "I should have kept this from happening. I should have stopped it, should have never put us or you in that kind of position. I should have been the person you told, who took care of you, this. How did I not know?"

Chelsea stroked his cheek again. "Not for lack of trying. We both knew there was more to the story, and you did everything possible to get answers and to the bottom of what was really going on."

Chelsea watched as Ben took a sharp breath.

"Oh, God," he whispered. "We and you didn't remember."

Chelsea's eyes widened, and she quickly got up and went to him. "No," she said sternly. "I don't feel bad about what happened between us, and I sure as hell don't want you to, either. I may not have had my memories, but you were exactly what I wanted. I have no regrets or ill feelings about that."

Chelsea maneuvered her way in front of him, her arms reaching to wrap around his neck, placing his own around her waist. She pulled him closer and closed her eyes when his head dropped against hers and she could feel his cool breath.

"Why aren't you yelling at me?"

Chelsea blinked, tilting back to look at him. "You still expect me to?"

"Yes," he said, tearing his eyes from her to look at the floor.

She didn't ask what he expected her to yell about, but assumed it was a combination of everything. Instead, she closed her eyes and leaned her head down to his chest.

"I don't want to yell at you anymore, Ben. I don't want to fight anymore. I was coming back here to see you because I wanted to clear the air. Because I missed you and I know you have spent all this time thinking had I woken up and seen you there at the hospital, that all hell would have broken loose if I remembered you, but it wouldn't have. I would have been so thankful you were there. And even with not remembering you or us, I was still thankful for you being there and for everything you did. After all the shit we went through, you still flew all the way out there and stayed by my side the entire time. You did everything in the world for me, when I am the last person who deserved that from you."

"You always deserve someone to be there and take care of you."

"Had I woken up with my memory right after the accident or when I was still in the hospital or anytime since then, I would have still been grateful for everything you've done for me. I still would have wound up in the same position, too. I would have fallen right back in love with you. This is just the way it happened, and I'm okay with that. Maybe this is exactly what we needed. You know, bad things leading to good places and all that."

"I wasn't trying to put my work in front of you," Ben said. His voice sounded hoarse.

Chelsea cuddled closer to him. "I know. Neither of us were. It was just a stressful time, and we weren't handling it very well. I see that a lot better now."

"Nothing happened with Veronica, Chels. I swear. Not with her or anyone else, ever."

"I know," she whispered back. She could feel tears stinging at the corner of her eyes again.

"I would have helped you with anything you needed after."

Chelsea looked up at him and cupped his cheek, causing one of those unshed tears to shake loose.

"I know you would have," she promised. "Part of me just didn't want to see sense or logic about anything."

"I didn't mean all those things I said to you afterward. I was just—I don't even know where all of that came from. I think part of me wanted to lash out, but also stupidly thought it would somehow help."

"I know. I didn't, either. I was in the same boat in a lot of ways. I didn't mean any of it."

Ben's forehead dropped down on top of hers. "I love you, Chelsea Sanders."

Chapter Thirteen

Ben had the sliding door to the balcony open as he looked out at the lights of the city. With a sigh, he flicked away the fourth cigarette he'd burned through tonight. He could count the number of times he smoked on fewer fingers than he had, but after all the shit today, it was needed.

Just a few seconds later, Chelsea's small, familiar frame pressed against his back, her arms circling around him from behind. "You're mad," she said over a heavy yawn, and he closed his eyes.

She knew him too well sometimes.

He took a deep breath. "Yes."

He was well beyond angry.

He heard her sigh, but nothing followed. He was furious at himself for the mess they were in, for Veronica, and for not straightening things out between them well before they spun out of control. He wasn't angry at her by any means for what happened to her, but he would be lying if he said he wasn't upset that she hadn't told him before.

He wished he could bring Mitchell Craft's useless corpse back to life just so he could put him right back in the ground. He wanted to hunt Veronica down and make her pay if she had a single thing to do with what her brother had done and honestly, a small part of that was there just on damn principle alone. He was angry for everything they lost, those months they spent fighting, the separation and finally, the divorce. There was so much time they would never get back. They should be building their life together, making memories.

They should have a family now, a little toddler running around.

Not this.

And Ben told her as much.

"I know," she whispered into his back.

His whole body ached, inside and out. His eyes hurt from tears he shed, and from ones he hadn't. His head hurt from all the damn thoughts he couldn't keep from running through one after the other. His chest hurt from the sucking wound of knowing how everything could have been and what they lost.

He always thought there was more to the story. There had to be, with how she had been behaving, but never in a million years would he have thought this. Just wanting to be out of the marriage and using the shit with Veronica as an excuse? Sure. Maybe her having had an affair and turning cover on him? Possibly. There being more to the story, more Veronica might have done or said that he wasn't aware of? Abso-fucking-lutely. But this? Never.

Never had his mind gone anywhere near this fucking catastrophe.

They stood there in silence for a long time, Chelsea hugging close to him from behind. He sighed, letting his hands cover hers across his stomach. "You're still wearing your ring," she said, feeling the cool metal.

He knew she'd noticed long before this moment, but she hadn't questioned him or brought it up. Ben's thumb instinctively went to the wedding ring, rubbing the band.

"I've never taken it off," he said, closing his eyes. He heard her sigh and felt her head switch from one cheek to the other against his back.

"I could never accept that we were really over," he said next. "And my heart still belonged to you, so I just couldn't take it off."

Chelsea was silent for a moment. "Me either. I tried more than a few times, but it never felt right. I would get angry or sad and practically rip the bands off of my hand and throw them or just set them to the side or whatever, but then I'd go frantically searching for them all over again."

Looking down, he only now even noticed she was wearing her engagement and wedding rings again. He couldn't deny the sight gave him a little skip in his heart.

"The hospital tried giving them to me when I arrived," he told her. "They said you had been wearing them, but they had to take them off at one point or another. Not knowing what would happen next, I just asked if there was a bag or something I could put your personal items in and left it at that."

It was a risk to leave something so expensive with the hospital, but at the time he had been worried that she would wake up and all hell would break loose. That he would end up taking off without giving them back to her.

"Are you mad that I told you?" she asked after another pause came and went.

Ben slipped her hands from around his middle and turned around to face her. "No," he said. "I'm glad that you told me what happened. I'm upset that you didn't tell me before, yes. But more than anything I just hate that you had to tell me that at all. And I wish I could go back in time and stop it from happening, or somehow make it right, now. But I just don't know what I can do, and I feel helpless here."

Chelsea's fingers intertwined with his as she took a step closer to him. "You've done more than you even realize already," she said. "I should have told you before, but I am glad that I finally did."

Ben dropped his lips down to her forehead briefly. "You should go back to bed."

"Will you lay down with me?" she asked.

"If that's what you want."

Chelsea gave him a small smile and nodded.

"Okay," he said and led her back inside, sliding the door shut. Ben buried his face into her hair, his arms wrapping around her and holding her close. "God, I missed this," he heard her say, and he couldn't have agreed more.

Ben blinked a few times as Chelsea stirred beside him. "Hey," he said, his voice rough from just having woken up.

"Is it still dark out?" she asked, laying her head down on his chest. She cuddled closer to him, one of her legs bending and curling on top of him.

"I have no idea," he said once she got comfortable.

Chelsea was quiet after that, her fingertips drawing random designs on his chest and arms. "Do you remember when I asked what you would change about us, if given a chance?"

"I remember."

"You said you would change the fact that we ever ended. Do you still feel that way? That we shouldn't be over?"

Ben swallowed. "Yes, at least from my point of view, that is how I feel."

She was silent again for several moments. "What if we weren't?"

He tilted his head a bit to look down at her. "What do you mean? What if we weren't what?"

Chelsea sighed, pulling herself off of him so she could sit up. "What if we weren't over? What if everything that happened recently really is some sort of second chance for us?"

Ben cleared his throat, following her lead and pushing himself up on one elbow. "Would that be something you would actually want?"

"I know we were a disaster before, but I don't want to think of that as how we ended things, either. I don't want this to be the end of our road. We were so much better than that and I think we could be again. I know that we would have a lot to work through, but I think that's a path worth taking."

Ben pulled himself the rest of the way up, sitting up against the headboard. He cleared his throat again. "A lot happened, Chels."

Her face fell. "I know. And I understand."

"Chelsea, you are still everything in this world I want, and there is nothing in this world I wouldn't give to be with you again if given a chance. But a lot happened with us, and I wouldn't want to relive that by any means. I wouldn't even know where to start."

She scooted a touch closer. "Maybe just by being together, being around one another? Working through what happened with us before, learning better ways to deal with problems that might arise in the future. Remembering what made us fall in love with each other in the first place?"

"And seeing where it all takes us?" he asked after a moment.

Chelsea nodded.

"Do you honestly think you could let go of the past enough for us to have a future?"

Chelsea took his hand. "I'm already there on some things. I look at you and see the man that I love, that I want to be with, that I want to make everything up to because I'm the real reason we're here now. I do trust you. Yeah, maybe that is something that needs to be worked on, but I do."

The two of them spent hours talking, only getting up to take a bathroom break or to grab a bottle of water to bring back. Though, when Chelsea's stomach wouldn't stop growling, Ben finally told her to get up. That he was finally going to fix them something to eat.

She grabbed his arm before he stepped into the hallway. "Ben?"

Ben reached a hand out, cupping her cheek. "I'm yours, Chelsea. I always have been, and I always will be. For as long as you want me."

"I do want to make this work, " she said.

He bent down to kiss her. "Then we'll find a way."

If it was the last thing he would ever do, he would make that promise true. He spent nearly two years doing nothing but wishing for this very opportunity, and he wasn't going to waste it.

"Just like that?"

Ben shrugged. "Like you said, it'll be a long road with a lot to work out, but if you honestly want to try, then, yeah. I'm in, just like that."

Chelsea smiled, standing on her tiptoes to kiss him again. Maybe they would get their happily ever after, after all.

Chelsea woke up before the alarm went off for a second time. She hadn't exactly been looking forward to her doctor's appointment before, but now she just felt uneasy.

Still, she couldn't help but smile as she looked over at Ben's sleeping face mere inches from hers. He had one arm draped across her, holding her tightly as he slept, cuddling her as if he was afraid she'd disappear. He was warm and comfortable. It felt like home being in his arms. Just like it always did.

Despite him having been honest about his feelings and for everything he'd done to show her how he felt, Chelsea still found herself surprised by how easily he agreed to a second chance happening between them.

He was upset, angry and hurt about, well, everything and he had made that clear, but he was handling things better than she expected. Had Mitchell Craft still been alive, Chelsea was sure it would have been a very different case. They both knew they couldn't just magically pick up where they left off. They had a beautiful relationship ruined once. That couldn't be erased. But they both wanted a future, wanted to give this a try. That was what she was holding onto.

She loved it all—waking up next to him, falling asleep in his arms, eating lunch and dinner together, just sitting around talking about what projects he was working on, filling one another in on those months they went without any contact, her plans for what she was hoping to do next.

It was more than she hoped to dream.

Chelsea laid there until the alarm went off, watching as Ben's eyebrows furrowed at the noise. When his eyes opened, he blinked a time or two before a slow smile crossed his face. Chelsea remembered the first time she witnessed this very thing happen. She could recall thinking how she wished she could wake up like this every day for the rest of her life.

Truth be told, she had the same thoughts as she looked at him now.

Ben took Chelsea to her appointment, waiting for her the entire time despite her protests of how boring that would be and reminding him that she could always text him when it was over. She actually debated asking him to come back with her, but that seemed like a bit much, so she just accepted him being there for her out in the waiting room.

"I promised Dannie, I would call her later to fill her in on everything, but after all of that, I think I might push that back until tomorrow," Chelsea said with a sigh.

"I bet she'll have quite a few questions. Might be best. You've had a lot going on the past couple of days."

Chelsea nodded. She'd briefly overviewed a few things with Danielle and Penny after she got her memories back. They stayed afterward, just talking to her and making sure she was okay. Chelsea promised that she would tell them everything. That there was so much more to the story than they were aware of. She promised to call them as soon as she spoke with Ben.

She thought maybe after telling Ben what happened with Mitch, it would be easier, but that wasn't entirely the case. She still had that same sense of dread when she thought about telling someone else.

Even her best friend.

She would get through it. Just maybe not tonight.

Chapter Fourteen

Chelsea held her breath as she entered the house, with Ben following close behind. Since she got her memories back, he had yet to make it past the foyer, despite the handful of dates they had been on. But she hoped tonight she would be able to convince him to stay.

When he wasn't around, she missed him terribly. Sure, they would spend hours on the phone and check in with one another via text, but it was never the same as having him right beside her. She hated when he was gone.

Chelsea felt her heartbeat quicken when she turned around, watching as he closed the door behind him. His eyes met hers and he gave her a hint of a smile before pulling her into his arms.

Both of them were still wet from their latest adventure, which involved swimming in a private, indoor and heated float pool. Chelsea tried to get a read on him. "Do you wanna take a shower?"

His head tilted so slightly that she wondered if she imagined it. His eyes bore into hers as he attempted to decipher whether or not she meant what he thought she did.

Which she very much did.

He seemed to understand that, tipping his head just the smallest bit toward the stairs.

When she turned around this time, Ben's hands went to her hips, pulling her closer. His lips met hers and her legs wobbled from the contact. He helped her out of her shirt, then her shorts. She slipped out of her shoes before grabbing for his wet shirt and together they pulled it off of him. As he got his own shoes off and put them off to the side, she reached into the shower and started the water.

Ben kissed her again. "I love you," he whispered, before pressing his lips to her forehead.

She smiled. "I love you, too."

Ben's hands went to the back of her neck, undoing the knot in her swimsuit top. "Let me see you."

Chelsea swallowed as he tossed the item over to the side with the rest of their wet clothes. She shimmied out of the bottom half, watching as Ben untied the string to his swim trunks.

Ben was one of the very few men she had ever seen naked, but it was a sight she would never get tired of. Her eyes lingered on his manhood, which was already at half-mast. She was reaching out to touch him before she even knew what she was doing, feeling the pulse between her legs grow stronger.

Ben moaned low in his throat but let her play. He gripped the edge of the countertop as he went from being half hard to twitching and jumping in her warm palm. "You're going to run out of hot water if you keep that up," he said, picking her up and carrying her through the glass door.

"I don't think I would mind that much."

Ben chuckled and walked her backward until she was under the warm spray. He watched in one hell of an intense gaze as she tilted her head, letting the warm droplets rain down.

Chelsea gasped, her eyes popping back open when she felt his large hands. She arched into his palms as he cupped her breasts, his thumb sliding over the pointed peaks. Ben closed the small space between them, turning and pressing her against the side wall. His hands trailed up her chest to her neck, cupping her flesh lightly between his hands as he kissed her until they were both panting and breathless.

"You are so fucking perfect," he whispered, kissing her again.

As he reached for her shampoo bottle, Chelsea found her arms moving on their own again, heading for the same place as before. Ben let out a shaky breath, pouring some of the foamy liquid from the bottle into his other hand. One of her hands braced against his lower abdomen, while the other slowly stroked and played with his thick cock.

She missed him in every way, and sex had certainly been one of them. After they split, the emptiness in that department was easier to deal with, but now he was all she could think about.

Ben helped rinse her hair and worked on his own while she lathered on her body wash. His eyes never left her, somehow growing darker by the second. He took no issue in helping her wash off again, either, taking the loofah from her and rubbing it against her skin.

It wasn't long before it was just his hands caressing her.

Chelsea sucked in a hard breath as he went from standing before her down to his knees. His eyes stayed trained on hers as he lifted one of her legs over his shoulder and his mouth found its way to her core. Ben smirked. A shudder ran through her entire body at the first touch of his tongue, her hands flying out to grab handfuls of his hair.

"Fuck, I love you."

Ben shut the water off when it turned cold. He picked her up, easily carrying her off to the bedroom. "Chels?"

"Hmm?"

"You sure about this?" he asked. "Because we don't have to do anything."

She pressed her mouth to his. "Trust me, I am beyond sure that I want this. That I want you."

He kissed her, then. "I don't think I'll be able to walk away afterward."

Chelsea smiled. "You think you could, anyway?"

"I don't know, but I would try. If that's what you truly wanted. But there's no coming back from this. Not for me."

"I don't want you walking away, now or ever. You are what I want."

The assault was also hanging in the air, but she was thankful he didn't bring it up. Instead, he muttered something about needing to run out to the car. "I only grabbed my phone and the keys. I need to get a condom."

She was more than a little tempted to tell him to just forgo wearing one but told him there were still some in the nightstand.

"Please," Chelsea answered the quiet question in his eyes, asking her one last time if she was sure about this. He kept teasing her opening, and she was going to combust if he didn't make a move soon.

Thankfully, he didn't make her wait long, just seconds later, she was stretching around him. Ben moved painfully slowly, making sure she felt every last inch of him. He kept repeating how much he loved her, how much he missed her, pressing deeper.

He was not taking her up on any of her hints to move harder or faster.

She groaned. "Ben!"

"What is it, my love?"

"You know what."

"Mmm," he said, flipping them so she was now on top. "Why don't you show me?"

Chelsea shot him a dark look as she stretched back, shifting her hips. His hands toyed with her breasts as she bounced up and down on his long cock, pinching and twisting her nipples between his fingers, squeezing the soft flesh in his palms. "So close," she said, squeezing her legs around him.

Ben didn't waste any more time teasing, flipping them once more. "Chels?"

Chelsea lifted her head, kissing him hungrily. This only increased when he pinned her arms. She still craved him holding her down and being the one to finish them off, and knew where the concern came from, but it was different with him. She loved the possessive side of him.

Desperate.

On edge.

Ben's other hand slipped between them, pinching and rubbing her clit. She didn't even have time to huff out a warning. Her back arched, and she cried out his name as her hips bucked. Unsure if she wanted him closer to her or if she should push away, her fingernails dug into his wrist as the tingling spark exploded and her entire body shuddered as Ben all but collapsed.

Once he had feeling back in his legs, Ben reluctantly pulled himself to his feet and went to the bathroom to clean up. He picked their pile of wet clothes up off the bathroom floor and carried them down to the washer. When he got back upstairs, he found Chelsea laid out in the bed underneath the blankets. "I do love you, Chelsea Sanders," he said, staring at her.

"*Black*," she corrected him again.

He didn't say it to her, but he still didn't feel right using his surname without them being married anymore. Instead, he just gave her a bit more of a smile before coming to join her in the large bed.

Chelsea immediately pillowed herself on top of him. "I love you, too, Ben. I always have."

When morning rolled back around, Chelsea once again found herself awake before his alarm went off. She sat up, turning over to look at his sleeping face. She had no idea how she would handle losing him again and had no intention of finding out. She cursed herself when his eyes opened, his hand coming up to brush away some stray tears that fell.

"Come on, now," he whispered. "Don't do that."

Chelsea shook her head, feeling ridiculous. "Sorry," she said, willing herself to get a grip. "I just hate knowing you're leaving and that I won't see you for a few days."

Ben gently brought her face to his, softly taking her lips. "I know, beautiful. I'm not much of a fan of it, either. But you sure as hell aren't making it any easier to pull myself out of this bed."

Chelsea chuckled just a little, rubbing her cheek against his. She really didn't mind the leaving part. It was how long he would be gone that had her wanting to blurt out something she shouldn't.

Ben did his best to make sure everything was alright before finally taking the steps out the front door. But it didn't make her miss him any less.

Ben felt like an ass as he drove back home. He knew Chelsea had no problem with him going into work, especially with the flexibility they were affording him, but hated that they still had so much time apart.

He didn't want to push or overstep any invisible lines. They were still in the early stages of fixing the damage they created, and he was treading carefully, for the most part.

So, he was rather shocked when Chelsea called him while he was getting dressed to head into the office and asked him to come home. It was how she said it that had him stopping mid-air, furrowing his eyebrows as he concentrated on the small phone in his hand.

"I know this is probably rushing things, but I hate when you're not here. I have been trying to deal with it and to let things just fall into place like they should on their own and everything but truthfully, I want you here." Chelsea took a deep breath. "I want you to move back home."

Ben swallowed. His world was spinning. "What?"

Another deep breath from her. "I know we still have things to figure out, to work through. But wouldn't it be easier to do that if you were here? And not only get through the past but already be working on the future for us in the process, too."

"I, uh." He sat down on the edge of his bed, looking around the room, unsure of what the hell was happening. "You want me to move back to Saltridge, back in with you?" he asked her after another moment passed.

"Yes," she said. "This was our home and I want it to be that again. And with us already having lost so much time over just stupid worthless things. I don't want to rush anything, but I don't want to miss out on anything, either, or waste any more time. I'd like to find a balance for all of that."

He was quiet for a long time. He could hear her nervousness.

"You think it's a bad idea," she said as he went to open his mouth. "Which, right, it probably is."

"Give me a few days. I'll get things straightened out up here and if you still want me there, I'll come back home."

Ben finished getting dressed, walked out into the living room of his condo, and looked around. For so long, he wished for her to tell him to come home but had long since given up on such a hope becoming reality. It made his head spin. The idea of calling their home his "home" again made his heart swell. The thought of going to bed next to her every night and waking up beside her every morning made his face light up like a damn Christmas tree.

He didn't know if it was the right play any more than she did, but he wasn't going to turn down the opportunity. If nothing else, he would work twice as hard to make sure they didn't fuck this up.

Chapter Fifteen

Chelsea couldn't believe that today was the day. She was a mess of nerves. Her stomach had been in knots ever since she woke up. It had been a week since she asked Benjamin to come home, and he was finally on his way.

Ironically enough, these last seven days were the longest time they had been apart since her accident. Apparently, arranging for your entire life to be transported ninety miles took time and patience. Something that she wasn't exactly blessed with.

At least not when it came to that damn man.

A part of her wanted so badly to pick up where they left off that night. Before Veronica's stunt, and before Mitch and her entire world crumbled. But that wasn't possible. The past was the past. It didn't matter how much either of them wished they could change it. All they could do now was look to the future. They had a long road ahead of them. One that hopefully led them to something even better than what they shared before.

That's what she kept trying to tell herself, anyway.

They deserved this. They could do this. With one last breath, Chelsea reached for the brass knob and pulled the heavy door open. Benjamin's eyes darkened as they both stood there drinking each other in. She opened her mouth to speak, to say something. Anything. But no words would come. It didn't matter, though, because Ben was just as speechless. The next thing she knew, his lips were pressing against hers, reminding her that sometimes they didn't need words.

As much as she wanted to stay right there wrapped up in his arms, the wind was picking up, a sure sign that a storm would be here soon. Still, Chelsea couldn't resist softly kissing him one more time. Ben smiled sheepishly when her fingertips slipped down his chest, then lower.

"Sorry," Ben said once he found his voice.

"Don't," Chelsea said, pressing a finger to his lips. She didn't want him to apologize. They had done enough of that. Her nerves were still frayed. There were still questions that needed answers, things they needed to figure out. But she spent enough time this week worrying. They had the rest of their lives for that. Right now, she just wanted to bask in their new beginning. "Welcome home, Ben."

It took tremendous strength, but Ben was finally able to step away from her on the porch. Once they were inside, however, a slight awkwardness overtook them once again. He'd spent a good portion of the last seven days trying to imagine this moment. How it would feel to walk back inside this house knowing that it was once again his home. Silently, he followed Chelsea into the living room. Everything was just as it had been the last time he was here, and yet something felt different.

"Okay," she said, noticing the small duffel bag he was carrying. "Either something got lost in translation or…?"

"I hired movers, the rest should arrive in a few days. I just didn't want… Well, I thought it best that I bring enough with me, so that there's no reason I need to go back there. To my apartment, I mean. I don't think I could take another night away from you."

With tears in her eyes, Chelsea nodded her head in agreement. "I think we've spent enough time apart."

Ben reached out to grab her by the hand. "Too much. But this doesn't mean that we have to rush anything, either. If you're more comfortable with me in the guest room for the time being I would understand."

Chelsea couldn't suppress the giggle that escaped from her. "Ben, you're not staying in the guest room. We've talked about this. I want you home. In our bed at home. I want to figure this out together, you and me. Which reminds me, there's something that I want to show you."

Ben followed her up the stairs to their bedroom. Their bedroom. Now that was going to take some getting used to. He still couldn't believe any of this was happening. He kept expecting to wake up back in his apartment with these last several weeks being nothing more than some torturous dream. He wasn't going to waste this chance, though. He definitely didn't have all the answers. Or any of them. All he knew for certain was that there was no way he would be able to walk away from her a second time.

He simply didn't have any willpower left.

His heart was hers.

One step after another, Ben followed closely behind her, pausing only for a moment before stepping across the threshold of what was once again their bedroom. As he looked around the familiar room, he felt a hard tug on his heartstrings. There were spaces throughout not only the bedroom, but the house itself that were now empty because of their separation. Most people wouldn't notice as he left nearly everything the night he finally walked out. But if he looked close enough, he could still spot the differences.

The empty bookshelves downstairs where he used to display his collection of first editions. His side of the sink in the bathroom. Bare walls where their pictures once hung.

At least their room looked more like it had before all hell broke loose between them. It was nothing major, but he did spot the bed, and he also noticed the Mr. and Mrs. matching mugs sitting back on their respective nightstands. The small corner shelf, which had been missing, was now hanging back on the wall with a few mementos from their wedding displayed atop it. Even the vase Danielle got them for their first anniversary was there.

Finally, the little sign about second chances and some framed photos of the very few she'd sneakily taken in the past several weeks hanging below it caught his eye. He might still be having a hard time wrapping his head around how they got here, but he would forever be thankful for this wild road that led them back to one another. There was nothing in this life he wanted more than to spend it with her.

He looked over at Chelsea and chuckled slightly at how nervous she suddenly looked. He walked over to her and kissed her gently. "I love it."

It reminded him of when he moved in for the first time. It didn't take long before his laptop and phone were sitting back on his nightstand, his clothes and the extra pair of shoes he brought squared away, Chelsea having taken his toothbrush and similar items off to the bathroom.

"So," Chelsea said when she returned, her small body leaning against the doorframe of the room. "This is real now, right? No turning back?"

Ben's face softened, and he held a hand out, pulling her to him once she got closer. "Never," he assured her.

Afterall, they had forever to figure this out.

Ben's kiss was slow, teasing, barely tasting her tongue before pulling away. He couldn't believe that he was really here, really home. His lips brushed the top of her soft blonde hair. This constant back and forth over whether they were moving too fast or not fast enough was exhausting.

Chelsea gasped as he lifted her up and guided her into the warmth of the enormous bed. Mouths and heartbeats were frantic. Her shirt lifted with a moan. Leaving the sweetness of her mouth, Ben licked and nipped on the soft flesh of her neck.

Ben dropped open-mouth kisses across her collarbone and chest and when Chelsea arched against him, he captured one of her hard nipples in the heat of his mouth. Chelsea's nails scratched down his scalp.

A soft whimper. A breathy moan. His name falling from her lips was always his undoing.

Ben left the soft comfort of her perfect breasts to continue taking in every inch of her bare body. Chelsea squirmed as his lips trailed down her lean stomach, biting lightly at her hip.

Chelsea propped up on her elbows as she watched him and seemed to hold her breath once he settled between her supple thighs. Their eyes stayed locked until she fell back against the bed. "Please don't make me wait."

Ben smirked. He never grew tired of pleasuring this woman and never would. She tasted like heaven and he still had a lot of fucking time to make up for.

Chelsea's hips bucked as he brought her closer and closer to the edge. This was his favorite game. There was nothing he loved more than watching her shudder and gasping on the verge of bliss. Well, almost nothing.

Chelsea nearly yanked his hair out as she pulled him back up to her.

"Hi," he tried to tease, but he barely got the word out before she pulled his head down to hers, kissing him roughly.

It was his turn to groan as her free hand snuck between them and grabbed his aching erection. She pumped her hand up and down his length before whispering how much she needed him. He made no move to stop her when she guided his engorged flesh to her entrance.

She wasn't on birth control. A fact that filled him with equal parts terror and excitement. There were a number of hoops to navigate before they crossed that bridge, but just the idea of the possibility was one hell of a high.

Ben was losing control, hips moving frantically. All these new, unobstructed sensations were leaving him overloaded. He couldn't get close enough to her, buried deep enough to satisfy this dizzying need. Chelsea's small body bounced, his name coming out in gasps and moans from her swollen lips, emerald eyes swirling with pleas to tip them over that edge into ecstasy.

He was about to leverage his body weight, but she beat him to the punch. His eyes damn near rolled back into his head as he stared down at her fingers rolling over her slick, swollen clit. He watched in fascination as she teased and twisted the bundle of nerves. It felt like an eternity, with time standing still, before he felt her warm walls flutter around him, her body jerking forcefully as she peaked.

"Fuck," he groaned. He was drowning in how wet and warm she was.

Chelsea's ass slapped against his thighs as he plunged into her, growing painfully as his hips slammed one last time.

"Jesus fucking Christ," he said once he could do something besides some heavy panting.

Chelsea laughed. "I did say that I missed you."

Chapter Sixteen

The second day, Ben attempted to work a full day and failed. They didn't even make it upstairs. Chelsea was in the kitchen, just about to grab a cup of coffee, when he stormed in, grabbing her by the waist and pinning her up against the fridge. They needed no words as he spun them, laying her back on the closest surface. He swiftly shed them of their clothes and lavished each inch of her wondrous expanse until she was a panting mess. Then nearly choked when Chelsea unexpectedly reached between them, her small fingers wrapping around his rigid flesh.

"Condoms."

Chelsea's brow furrowed, and she let out a small pout. "I hate them."

Ben smiled. "I know," he said, dropping a quick kiss. "So do I."

"They're also upstairs."

Ben groaned. How convenient.

Chelsea hadn't come out and said it, but he knew where that pretty little head of hers was. Just the thought of her pregnant with his child made him ache with a need he couldn't explain. He was also just as aware of what a dangerous game they were playing. But it sure was hard to worry about such things when they were like this. Especially when she was so fucking wet, and warm and nothing if not intent on pushing him to his absolute limit.

Ben dug his fingers into the supple flesh of her ass as he positioned himself against her dripping entrance. Eyes rolling back, he took a steadying breath before thrusting inside her scorching heat. Nothing compared to this, and after everything they had been through, nothing ever would.

The table creaked. Either Ben didn't notice or simply didn't care, because despite her weak warning, he only moved faster. Her stomach twisted as the fire inside her built until it was nearly unbearable. Legs locked around him, she matched him move for move, but it wasn't enough.

Ben was teetering. She knew his tells. Any other time, she might see how long she could torment him, knowing he would do everything in his power to make sure she got there first. But she was just as close.

Ben hissed through clenched teeth. "Fuck." Once again, his thumb rolled over her sensitive bundle, circling and teasing for just a few seconds before breaking down and giving into her small cries. "Now," he said, finally releasing her arms as he trailed down to give one of her pebbled pink nipples a gentle squeeze. "Come for Daddy."

Somehow, one evening in the blissful aftermath of their lovemaking, Chelsea convinced Ben to pull it together long enough for a movie night with her friends. It was a terrible idea. He hadn't even been back in the house for a week yet, and he was nowhere near ready to share her. But he was never very good at telling her no, and that hadn't changed. Plus, he knew she missed her friends, having been living so many states away. So with great reluctance he agreed, but only after she promised that this little movie night wouldn't turn into some marathon lasting until morning.

According to Nate, it was his turn to pick the movie. Chelsea wasn't sure how he had come to that conclusion since she hadn't been around for the last several months, but not only was she not up for any arguments, she honestly didn't care what they watched. She was just happy to have everyone she cared about under the same roof. Besides, if it was too scary, she could always cuddle up to Ben and let the rest of them fade away.

If there was anything she craved after these last few years, it was some sense of normalcy. As much as she was enjoying spending every moment with Ben, eventually they had to do something besides each other. Even if it did feel a little torturous.

She desperately wanted everyone to accept her and Ben as a couple again. Of course, Danielle and Penny already welcomed him back with open arms. It was almost as if they were able to just pick up where they left off.

Almost.

Nathaniel was going to take some work. It took years for him and Ben to bond the first time around. Nate wasn't exactly the most understanding, and he'd never been great at forgiving or forgetting anything.

"So, what?" Nate said, glancing at her and Ben as he reached for another slice of pizza. "He helps you regain your memory, and suddenly you're married again?"

Danielle's eyes widened. "Nate!"

Nate shrugged. "*What?* It's the truth."

Chelsea's face was on fire. As much as she loved Nate, sometimes he could be a real asshole. "No one is getting married. At least not anytime soon," she added softly.

The next morning, after Ben left for work, Danielle surprised Chelsea with breakfast. She had a few days off since she and Penny were back on the hunt for a house.

"I apologized to Ben this morning. You know, for Nate."

Danielle looked up from her laptop and made a face. "What'd he say?"

Chelsea rolled her eyes. "*For his existence?*" she said, doing an impression of Ben.

The redhead chuckled at that. "Oh, well, you know Nate was witness to the two of you in your worst moments more than anyone else, I think. You know he's not the type to fall in line. He's not going to accept all of this as easily as the rest of us."

Chelsea sighed. "I know, and I was just thinking about that yesterday. It probably doesn't help that I haven't really told him the whole story of what happened, what led to Ben and me splitting up in the first place. Nor have I really sat and explained where my head was when I had the accident and everything."

"Nate doesn't know?"

Chelsea sighed again. "No. I also told Ben that this morning. He said it was my choice of who I let know about what Mitch did. Which it is, but I feel like Nate deserves to know, too. Especially with how he's been acting. He still sees everything as Ben did this, that and the other, without really having the full scope of what went on. Sometimes it gets on my every last nerve with all his digs at us or his mutterings about Ben, but then again, maybe it's good to have someone stopping us for a moment and questioning what in the hell is happening here. It is a lot to wrap one's head around."

Danielle tilted her head. "Penny and I just want you to be happy. We know that you and Ben had one hell of a rough go the first time you were together, and we know trying to work things out can't be easy but—"

"No, no!" Chelsea said. "I'm so thankful that you guys are okay with this. Don't get me wrong. It's just sometimes I worry we're getting too far ahead of ourselves, wanting things to just be right again. I know I do," she said. "Nate's questioning of us is a little grounding, I guess. Lindsey, too."

"Oh?"

"Well, he called me once. A video call."

"Linds isn't keen on you and Ben being back together?" Danielle asked, a little surprised.

"I wouldn't say that. He called, and he flirted, as he does, and he asked me how I was doing and all. It was just the way he said a few things that were kind of haunting. It was like he was begging me not to break Ben's heart again without saying the actual words. I just want us to be together, and it's like a sucker punch to the heart to even imagine things not working out. I don't think I could survive losing him again. And at the end of the day I know Lindsey is incredibly happy for us but he's worried."

"Nate is, too, you know."

"Yeah, I know. He's not being a jerk just to be one."

"You guys have so many people who love you both and who remember how happy and how perfect you were together for so long, and we only want what is best for you. People show that in different ways, sometimes. Although, there's no sense in constantly dwelling on the bad, either. Focusing on fixing what got you there in the first place and moving forward really is all you can do. Not everyone has to understand that, just you and Ben."

Chelsea sighed, laying her head down on the counter. "Sometimes that's easier said than done, though. Even for me. This middle ground we're in right now just kind of sucks. I mean, hallelujah for this honeymoon phase, but there's so much lurking underneath the surface we're going to have to get to at some point." Chelsea looked down at her hand. "Like, I hate not being his wife. Maybe it's just a piece of paper to some people, but it feels like something is missing to me. I mean, I'm trying to just enjoy dating again and knowing we're together, but there's just so much I wish we could have right now."

Danielle came and sat closer to her. "You'll get there, Chels. There's no rush, even if you feel like there is right now. You have the rest of your lives to get everything you both want."

Chelsea sighed again. They had been careless in bed, and frankly, everywhere else, several times since coming back into one another's lives. She knew that was the logical side of things, but it still didn't tame the gnawing feeling inside her. That feeling of living more in the future than the present while still trying to fix the past.

Ben closed the door to his office. It seemed like everyone needed something from him which he guessed was to be expected with as much time as he had been out of the office. Still, it was exhausting.

Releasing the breath, he felt like he'd been holding since he arrived this morning, he discarded his briefcase on top of his large oak desk. Loosening the tie around his neck, he pressed a button on his phone, telling his secretary to hold all of his calls.

Nate's comment about marriage stuck in his mind, not because he cared about his opinion but because he wasn't completely wrong. A big part of him knew what Nate meant and understood the ridiculousness of their situation.

Ben sat at his desk and tried to clear his mind for a few minutes before letting out a huge sigh. He rubbed his eyes then got up to make himself yet another cup of coffee. While doing that he noticed his neglected calendar hanging on the wall and decided to grab the closest marker and cross through some of the things he'd already taken care of. Noticing what day of the week it was, an idea suddenly struck him.

He couldn't deny his own excitement at the small gesture.

It was only flowers, but it was one tiny piece of their life that he could give back to her now.

Chapter Seventeen

"You remembered," were the first words he heard after picking up the phone.

"I remember everything about us," he told her softly. When he didn't get a response, he said a soft, "Hey," into the phone. Then, when she still didn't respond, and he heard her sniffle, he finally said her name.

"I love them," she eventually managed.

"Well, I'm glad," he told her, his voice still as gentle as possible.

"I just miss you."

Ben sighed. "I miss you, too, beautiful. Do you want me to come home?"

"Yes," she said, letting out a huge sigh herself. "No. I mean, I do, but you need to be there right now. I think I can make it a few more hours. *Maybe*."

"Want me to bring something home?"

"Nope! I'm going to surprise you with dinner tonight."

Ben chuckled. "You are?"

"I am."

"I will act completely shocked."

"You had better."

Everything in Ben's hands fell to the floor when Chelsea launched herself into his arms as he stepped through the door. She wasted no time, moving her hand to the front of his black pants while he kissed her long and slow. Ben groaned as she guided his hardening cock out of his pants and slid a condom on. Then groaned again when he found her wearing absolutely nothing underneath the skirt she had on.

"Hi," Chelsea said once he was inside her.

"Hi," he echoed.

After some of their immediate needs were met, and both of them got cleaned up, Ben followed through with his promise to remain surprised at the meal Chelsea prepared. "I figured we were eating out a lot and maybe getting back to some of our formerly normal routines would be nice," she said as they sat down.

Ben told her that his new work schedule was almost fully worked out so that should help. Waterstone had been good to him over the years. It was home in many ways, but if it ever again impaired their relationship, he would happily wave goodbye and find something else. His higher ups were working with him as much as possible, trying to make sure he had a good balance between everything he needed to do.

"I still have no idea what I even want to do," Chelsea told him. "I was looking through online job listings earlier to see what new jobs are in the area."

"If you want to," he replied. "I don't want you pushing yourself too much. You are still recovering. If anything, maybe focus on finding something part time for a while. I don't think I'm ready to share you with a classroom full of teenagers yet."

Chelsea playfully rolled her eyes at him. "Yeah, yeah. I know. But I feel so restless just fiddling around here all day, especially when you're not here."

"You could always be my assistant."

Chelsea shot him a look. "And what do you need assistance with?"

Ben just winked at her.

Much later in the evening, when Ben crawled into bed, Chelsea found her body melding easily against his. "What are you over here sighing about?" he asked her.

Chelsea nodded toward the phone in her hand, and he peered over her hair before asking to see it. She handed it over as he rolled onto his back, so she flipped to her other side, pillowing her head against his chest. "There's only been one I've seen and liked. I keep coming back to it, but I don't know."

He looked down at her as she sighed again. "It's teaching a few hours at a preschool during the week."

He smiled. "You'd be perfect for that."

Chelsea looked elsewhere in the room. "Yeah. Maybe. I just worry I'll be constantly reminded of what we could have right now if things were different. Or worse that it will all just make me wish we were working on having a baby right now."

Chelsea felt him pull her closer to him, dropping a kiss on the crown of her head. Her eyes closed, and she cursed the tears that formed and fell slowly onto his skin. "Come here," he said.

Her phone was placed off to the side as he lifted her up to him, her nose now brushing against his. "I really want a baby with you," she whispered.

Ben kissed her, his lips barely brushing against hers. "I know," he said. "And I promise you that we are going to make a family."

"But not right now."

Chelsea knew the timing wasn't right. How many times this week did she have this exact conversation with herself?

"The second we have this mess sorted out."

Chelsea wiped her eyes. "But I don't know when that will be. I don't know how to get us there."

He kissed her again. "I don't either, Chels. If I had a road map or a list of directions saying do A, B, C, D, and everything will be back to the way it should be, then I would be blowing through that fucker at record speed. But we don't have that. We just have to keep trying to figure it out as we go. Together."

Chelsea felt more tears coming and wiped them away. Sometimes, the past felt like it was crushing her. And just as often, the unknowns of the present felt like it was crushing her, too.

Ben's eyes burned as he struggled to control his own emotions. "Shhh, baby. Please," he whispered into her hair, but she only buried her face against his neck. His hands slipped beneath the shirt she was wearing, which he noticed was actually his, to trace a soothing path up and down her sides. "After I finally left, I used to have these dreams. Though I'm not even sure I would call them that."

Her tears softened as she listened to him speak. Shifting so she could see him better, she settled in the crook of his arm, her leg splayed across his lower half, clutching onto him as though he may disappear.

"What were they?" she asked. "Your dreams. What were they about?"

He wasn't sure if telling her any of this would help either of them, but he needed her to know that she wasn't alone. "Us. You. The family we would never have."

He felt her stiffen slightly. Even before her accident, he rarely let himself think about the weeks leading up to their divorce, or those first months after. He still wasn't sure how he ever survived those dark days.

"I know we weren't explicitly trying to get pregnant in those last days. But we weren't being careful. You weren't taking your birth control, and I definitely wasn't taking any measures to prevent something from happening. Those last few weeks between us were tense. We only made love a handful of times, but still." He shook his head. "I clung to that possibility for way too long."

Chelsea worked her lip between her teeth. After Mitch, the thought had occurred to her about the possibility of pregnancy. Though she didn't have daydreams. She had nightmares. There wouldn't have been any way for her to know if the baby was Ben's or a reminder from that night. Thank God it never came to that, but it broke her heart even more to know that was exactly what Ben was wishing for.

"A surprise pregnancy was the absolute last thing we needed, and I knew that then, too. But I didn't care about logic. Of course, knowing what I do now about Mitch, I'm so glad that's not something you had to go through." He sighed deeply. "I guess what I'm trying to say is that I understand what it's like to want something so badly you don't care about the consequences."

Chelsea cupped his cheek in her palm until he finally gave in and turned towards her. Neither of them said a word as she inched closer to his soft lips. It didn't matter if she got fifty more years with him, she would never get tired of kissing this man.

"So," she said, as a mischievous smile spread across her face. "What you're really saying is that if we were to accidentally get pregnant, then we could get married again and live happily ever after?"

Ben chuckled as he flipped them over. He pinned her beneath him as he nibbled down her neck. "We will have a baby," he said softly. "Maybe not this year, but we will get back there. There are just some things we need to take care of first."

Chelsea tilted her head so she could get a better look at him.

"Like?"

Ben grinned. "Like the small detail of being divorced. I think we should work on rectifying that before we make any decisions about babies."

He held her gaze, letting his words sink in.

She watched his eyes darken as a myriad of emotions flashed through them. Hadn't she just tried explaining to Danielle that she couldn't stand the fact that she wasn't his wife, even if it was only a legality. She softly traced along the ridge of his brow. "I think we just figured out our first step."

Ben let out a deep sigh as he settled back above her.

"You sure you want to be my wife again?"

"More than sure."

Chapter Eighteen

Ben's fingertips drummed on his desktop as he stared aimlessly at the wall. His mind was not in his work today. He was thankful he had some time between meetings to just do a whole lot of nothing. He heard his phone let off a little "ding" and reached over to grab it, grinning at the text.

"Maybe y'all need some sort of self-help book or something. *Remarrying Your Ex For Dummies*, perhaps?"

Lindsey's text made him chuckle.

Ben set the phone back down and shook his head. If only. He was beyond elated that both he and Chelsea were on the same page about what they wanted. But getting from one step to the next sent his mind reeling.

He didn't want to rush into it. Well, that wasn't true. But he also wanted to make sure their mistakes of the past would not be repeated. Ben needed her to know that she was it for him, that she always would be.

No matter what.

Then, on the other side of that was the fact of how in the hell you even go about marrying someone a second time. His brain would hurt if he even thought about any of it for too long.

He would look down at his wedding ring or at hers and wonder if he was supposed to get a new set. He loathed that idea, though. His ring hadn't left him once, and he didn't think he could bear to part with it. Getting them professionally cleaned prior to any such occasion or something he could deal with. Thinking about their rings would always have his mind wandering back to proposals. Finding the perfect ring could be tricky when she already had it. He felt like he'd done the perfect proposal already, too, so he had no idea how he'd make it special when the day did come.

He already gave her the dream wedding she wanted. It was beautiful and perfect. You couldn't exactly recreate that.

A courthouse wedding didn't seem to justify their journey, either.

He really had no idea what Chelsea might want for the day. He knew he'd be on board with anything she wanted, though. Bigger and better, small and intimate—anything was fine with him as long as she was happy, and it truly happened at the end of the day. He thought about the timing a lot, too. They already had an anniversary date, one Chelsea had been dead set on from the first time he proposed. He wondered if they should keep the same day or pick a new one. It was one question after another when he let his mind really go there.

He'd counted the days and weeks to what was once his favorite day more times than he'd like to admit. He didn't want to put pressure on either of them to get their acts together by then, but he also hated the idea of the date passing them by and having to wait another year if they decided to keep their previous wedding day the same.

Ben sighed, rubbing a hand down his face. "I'm getting too damn far ahead of myself," he said out loud to the otherwise empty room.

Chelsea's eyes fluttered to the clock once again, then back to her laptop. She didn't know which was worse, being anxious about meeting up with Nate for lunch or trying to fill out her resume for the preschool position. She studied the requirements, the description, everything she could about the job offered and the school itself before she put her resume under the magnifying glass one last time.

Letting out a deep breath, she hit send, then closed the laptop and looked at the time again. She was about to grab her phone and check on Nate when she heard the familiar rumbling of his truck. She used to tease him over the fact you could hear him roaring down the road from a mile away, but it became a thing of comfort over the years.

She quickly pulled their sliders out of the oven where she had left them to keep warm before making her way to the door. "Hey, Nate," she greeted as she opened the door, a smile on her face as she pulled her friend in for a big hug.

"The Chelster! I always feel like it's been years when I see you anymore."

Chelsea asked him how he was as she stepped out of the way to let him join her inside. He rubbed his hands together and his eyes wandered around the living area and up toward the stairs as he answered.

"He's not here," Chelsea said as she rolled her own eyes at him. "Ben is at work. *In LA.*"

"Just making sure," he replied. Shutting his eyes, he breathed deeply, smelling the air. "Hmmm, smells like yummy goodness. Lead the way, my lady."

Chelsea shook her head at his antics, leading the way into the kitchen as she tried to prepare herself for what was about to come.

Chelsea sat on the couch, wrapped up in her favorite blanket. Ben would be home soon, but she just couldn't pull herself together. She picked up her cell and quickly put an order in for pizza. Hopefully he wouldn't mind takeout again.

Her thoughts were still on Nate, and their earlier visit. As she expected, the conversation wasn't an easy one. She definitely didn't enjoy reliving the Mitch parts, but at least now he knew.

Nate had apologized to her, telling her what everyone else did. That he wished she would have confided in him, that she shouldn't have had to go through something like that alone. That he was sorry, and had he known he would have been more supportive. He admitted that Ben was still far from his favorite person, despite everything, but he vowed to at least try to be civil.

Then, in true Nate fashion, he jumped right to the tough questions, the Ben related ones. The ones about the future. The ones that she wished she had the answers to. The best she could give him was that they were trying, that they had goals, and that as far as she was concerned, Ben was going to be part of her life, forever.

The unanswered questions about their future had her sulking in her favorite pajamas that afternoon. She was glad Ben finally opened up last night. At least now they both knew they wanted to end up in the same place. She just wasn't sure if they were working on the same timeline, and she had so many questions.

Chelsea's eyes snapped open. She couldn't believe she hadn't heard him come in. The last thing she wanted was for him to find her like this. She wasn't even sure how long she had been crying. She sort of just spaced out.

She quickly wiped the tears from her eyes and attempted to sit up. "I'm sorry."

Ben looked furious. No matter how he tried to hide it, the anger always poured from his eyes. "What happened? What in the hell did that little woodworking asshole say?"

Confused, it took her a second to realize that he was talking about Nate. "No," she said, shaking her head. "This isn't about Nate. He didn't do anything, I swear."

"Then, what is it?"

"I'm sorry," she repeated, crying harder.

"For what?"

Chelsea took a shaky breath. "For everything."

Ben pulled her into his lap. "Chelsea, we've been through a lot of this," he told her softly. "I'm not blaming you for anything. There is an endless fucking list of things I wish I could go back and do over. Things I wish I handled differently. There were a number of things I did that wound up tearing us even further apart."

Chelsea hiccupped. "I should have just believed you, Ben."

He sighed, his eyes closing. "You have no idea how much I wish you would have," he said.

"It was all just so much at once."

"I know, baby," he whispered.

Chelsea's arms circled around him as she slid across his lap. "Walking Nate through everything just reminded me how screwed up our lives are, and how I had no idea how to fix this mess we're in."

Ben's thumb instinctively went to his wedding ring. "It seems like we have a lot of the same fears and worries," he said. "Perhaps after tonight we can finally put some of them to rest. It's one thing to know we want to get married again or that we want to have a child together, but it's a little unsettling trying to figure out things like—"

"How to marry the same person again?"

He nodded. "Exactly."

Chapter Nineteen

Chelsea's heart was racing hard. "I think you start with the asking part," she said once he confessed that he reached out to Lindsey just this morning for any advice he might have.

He almost smiled. "Yeah, probably so."

"Sometimes guys even get down on one knee to do it. And you're in luck because I just so happen to already have the perfect ring for you to use."

Ben just smirked as he continued to stare at her. Even after all this time, there were still moments where she took his breath away. Leaning forward, he gently captured her lips, but unlike before, he took his time lightly exploring the cavern of her mouth as if they hadn't done this ten thousand times before.

Her fingers threaded through his hair, pulling him closer, which only edged him further. His hands traveled from her thighs to around her waist so that he could hold her tighter. She was right, they already did everything perfect the first time. He didn't need to stress over some grand plan in order to ask her to be his wife again. He just needed to ask her.

When they finally broke apart, he forced himself to

take a steadying breath. Nose to nose, he whispered for her to open her eyes.

Chelsea's long lashes fluttered open, then almost as if she could sense where his head was, she tightened her hold around him. Her fingers wound tightly through the small hairs at his nape.

Even after all of the nights he spent bargaining with the universe for a second chance, he never thought he would get this.

He was completely aware that he didn't deserve this, and yet he was powerless to stop the words from spilling out.

"Marry me."

Chelsea gasped.

"I know I should probably get down on my knee," Ben said. "But I've already done that, and in my opinion that time was perfect. Besides," he added softly. "You're kind of already wearing your ring, and I don't want to cheapen anything we had by trying to recreate it. You're it for me, Chels. For better or worse. I'm tired of this limbo that we've been stuck in, I know this is fast, but I'm ready to move forward with my life. I'm ready to start my life with you. Again."

There was never a moment she had ever loved him more than that very second.

"Yes. Ben, absolutely, yes," she whispered before pressing her lips back to his. "You're right," she said, her head shaking against him. "We've already had the perfect wedding, the extravagant honeymoon and everything else. I don't care about centerpieces, or what the venue looks like. Being able to call you my husband again is the only thing that matters."

And there it was, that megawatt smile that she rarely got a glimpse of.

He was still beaming as he pulled her to him again in a kiss.

Chelsea’s lungs burned, but she didn’t pull away. She wished this night could be stretched out so that it never ended. They didn’t need silly things like oxygen or food. Maybe death by pleasure wouldn’t be everything she imagined, but it would still be one hell of a way to go.

"When?"

Ben’s eyes popped open. "When what, beautiful?"

Chelsea’s fingers traced a path down his nape, around his jaw, then over stubble on his neck, landing finally on the collar of his shirt.

"When do you want to get married?” she asked as the first button gave way. “I mean, we kind of need a timeline. That's the whole point, right?"

"Our anniversary?” he asked through clenched teeth. “I thought that was what you would want. If it's not, then we can pick some other day. Right now, in this second, I'd marry you tonight, Chels. If that's what you really felt was right."

His shirt was now fully open, and she pushed it off his shoulders, watching as it cascaded down.

"Our anniversary is perfect. I couldn't imagine having to choose a new one.”

Ben watched through hooded eyes as she kissed his shoulder, slowly making her way towards his ear. As expected, she paused to nip at the sensitive flesh, causing his cock to swell even further.

"You do realize that leaves us with less than ninety days, right?"

Ben made some strangled noise in the back of his throat, which she could only assume was in acknowledgement.

"Does this mean we can start trying again? Three months isn't very long."

That pulled him from his lust-filled haze.

"I know, I know," she said before he could respond. "It's irresponsible. And we would be rushing past a whole lot of things. But I dunno. I guess having a baby just feels like the first big step in getting us back to where we're supposed to be."

He really was trying to do the right thing. This wasn't some flippant topic but fuck if it wasn't the last thing he wanted to talk about. In fact, he didn't want to talk about anything. What he wanted was to make love to his newfound fiancée, but clearly this was something she wasn't budging from.

The next three months were going to be one hell of a testament to his resolve.

Ben groaned. "Can we please postpone this conversation? I know a baby is top priority, I do. But I think one life altering decision is enough for a day, don't you?"

Chelsea kissed him briefly before leaning back enough to flash him a sweet smile.

"Sure, but I'm not certain I remember where the condoms are. I guess you're just going to have to go upstairs and find one."

Ben's eyes narrowed, but her smile only grew brighter as she returned to her taunting. Her small hands felt like silk gliding down his chest. It was well beyond tempting to bury himself in her, just agree and let the fates figure it out, but one of them had to be fucking reasonable, so he stood up before she could unzip his pants.

Chelsea gasped at the sudden movement.

Ben walked them from the couch to one of the bookshelves in the room. He fiddled around blindly as his lips pressed against hers again. One hand searching while the other held her close until his fingertips finally found what he was looking for.

Ben pulled the hidden package out and smirked.

Chelsea's eyes narrowed. "Why exactly is there a condom hiding amongst the books and pictures and other lovely things on the shelf in our living room?"

"For shit like this.".

Chelsea huffed, but he only smiled, bringing his head back down and giving her a playful kiss.

"Soon," he whispered.

It didn't take long to get her to stop pouting about the lack of baby making and more interested in practicing for when the time came.

At least for the time being.

Ben smoothed his hands from her bare bottom up to her shoulder blades, relishing the way she arched into his touch. Her whole body seemed to lean back toward him as he followed the same path back down.

Ben took his time as he entered her, not thrusting until her tight walls fluttered in protest. Each time, he pulled away before thrusting deeper, settling into a steady rhythm of insertion and withdrawal.

Chelsea's head fell back, and she moaned, "More," each time he filled her. Which was almost enough to send him careening over the edge.

Unable to continue teasing her because of his fear of ushering this show into an early ending, Ben grabbed both of her hips, holding her still.

Chelsea moaned his name when he throbbed angrily inside of her. Hands gripping the back of the sofa, she did her best to balance on her tiptoes as high as she could.

Ben held this position before finally pulling back as he truly began thrusting in and out of her slick heat. His grunts of pleasure echoed through the otherwise quiet house, mixing in with her breathless chanting of his name as they moved together.

Chelsea's fingertips were nearly white from clawing into the couch, her ass bouncing against him with every move until he felt her begin to stiffen and shake.

"Oh, fuck," she whispered just before one of his hands snuck around to help push her over the edge.

Chelsea wiggled against his fingers working her clit as hot lava replaced the blood in her veins. Everything went dark and a loud scream ripped just as she began jerking happily beneath him.

When she caught a glimpse of herself in the mirror, Chelsea couldn't help but smile brightly. She was still on a high from their lovemaking for sure, but she was glowing because of something bigger tonight. She really hadn't expected Ben to ask this early on and certainly not tonight, but it was perfect.

"You are without question the most beautiful woman on the fucking planet," Ben whispered as she met him back downstairs. His lips teased her neck for a moment, his arms wrapping around her.

"I see you found dinner," she said, spotting the pizza in one of his hands against her.

"Mmhmm. I was starving."

She could agree with that. Ben kept his arms around her as she moved around the kitchen, grabbing a plate for herself and then led him back to the couch where he pulled her right back onto his lap.

"I love you," he told her softly.

Chapter Twenty

"There's something I need your guys' help with," Chelsea said, trying hard not to smile as she looked across the table.

She and Ben had spent the last two days in blissful seclusion, thanks to him being able to work from home. She enjoyed getting to bask in their enjoyment privately, celebrating with only each other. But now that the reality that they were actually getting married had time to sink in, the stress of planning everything was weighing on her.

They had less than three months to pull this off.

She needed help, fast.

Just before everyone was due to arrive, Ben volunteered to make a grocery store run. He wanted to pick up a few things to grill, plus he knew Chelsea would appreciate a few minutes alone with her friends to tell them the news. He just hoped Nate behaved himself.

Between bouts of making love the other night, while they were scouring the kitchen for food, Chelsea had jokingly mentioned that one of the things she missed most were his burgers. When she questioned him about having everyone over today, he thought it was a great idea. Plus, it would provide him the perfect opportunity to flip a few patties on the new grill he left behind.

He had already grabbed the meat and selected a variety of veggies for kabobs. The last thing he needed was buns. Making his way down the aisles, he passed by the pharmacy and carelessly tossed condoms into the cart. He must not have been paying attention, because when he went to turn around, he nearly knocked right into someone.

Just as he was about to apologize, he did a double take, not believing his own eyes. He stood staring, utterly speechless.

The blonde woman's eyes quickly cut down to the box of condoms in the basket, and back up to his own.

Her lips twisted. "So, I guess it's true, then. You really did go crawling back to her."

Anger flooded his veins.

His eyes narrowed as he took a step back.

"What are you doing here, Veronica?"

As soon as Chelsea said that she needed help planning a wedding, the room exploded. Not literally, but almost. Danielle jumped to her feet, running around the table to embrace her friend. Tears fell down her cheeks as she told Chelsea how happy she was for her, and Ben, too.

Penny was less enthusiastic, but still smiled and congratulated her.

Chelsea looked over to Nate who was oddly quiet. Even though she felt they made some progress through their conversation the other day, she was still a little worried what his reaction would be.

He was staring at the table between them, his knuckles lightly drumming a nervous beat on its edge. After what felt like an eternity, he finally looked up, his expression unreadable.

"Does this mean I get to plan the bachelor party again?"

Chelsea beamed. His acceptance meant more to her than he would ever know. There were still miles to go between him and Ben, but this was definitely a start. Walking over to him, she waited for him to stand before embracing him in a tight bear hug.

"Thank you, Nate."

Soon enough they were all deeply vested in the planning process as wedding venues were thrown around, dress ideas, and guest lists. Nate wouldn't stop mentioning Vegas. Danielle kept suggesting Europe, and Penny eventually chimed in saying that something simple might be better since they were on limited time.

Which only launched Nate into another spiel on the benefits of Vegas.

When they heard Ben pull into the driveway, everyone stood slightly shocked as Nate walked out to help him carry everything in. Not wanting to intrude on some special moment, the girls hung back in the house, though Chelsea may have taken a peek or two out of the blinds, just to make sure they weren't killing each other.

Before Ben could set all of the bags down, Chelsea walked up to him, pressing her lips to his. Even though his hands were full, he kissed her with reverence, backing against the kitchen island.

The sound of someone clearing their throat caught their attention, causing Ben to take a step back as Chelsea peered over his shoulder to glare at Nate, who quickly set his bags down and exited the room.

Raising her hands, she playfully pushed Ben towards Nate and the living room. "Go, now. Before we really embarrass our friends."

Stealing one more quick kiss, he left her to sort through the bags, as he walked into a room with an ecstatic Danielle.

As she was putting up the groceries, Chelsea couldn’t help the smile that spread across her face. She was truly happy for the first time in years. She couldn't believe how quickly everything was falling into place.

When she got to the last bag, she couldn’t help but smile as she pulled out the hamburger buns and set them on the counter. She knew he was doing this for her, cooking her favorite. She couldn't believe he even remembered what she said the other night. They had both been nearly delirious.

Taking out the last item, she couldn't help but laugh at the irony of the situation. Here she was finally coming to terms with their present, only to go and pull these damn condoms out of the bag.

Without another thought, she quickly dropped the sealed box inside the trashcan before pulling the bag out and tying it up.

"Be right back," she said over her shoulder. "Just taking out the trash…"

Danielle and Penny sat with Chelsea at the table. The two women were still throwing around different ideas for the upcoming wedding. The girls were absolutely on board with her and Ben not wanting to go all out this time and were giving her great motivation.

Chelsea teased Nate about when he and Holly would be getting married and that was part of what brought on the overpowering moment. He'd gone wide eyed and stuttered, which Ben then started teasing him about, too, and somehow the two just relaxed after that. They were off in the living room, and for the first time in forever, they were getting along. Hell, they were even talking without glaring at one another.

Ben waited until he knew Chelsea was asleep before making his way downstairs and slipping outside. He dialed Lindsey's familiar number and waited for the cowboy to answer as he took a seat on one of the wicker chairs by the fire pit.

When Ben asked what he would be doing on a certain date, Lindsey went quiet for a moment.

"I don't know, Ben. What *will* I be doing?"

"Well, I was hoping you could come out this way and do a little repeating of history."

"Yeah? You ask that girl to marry you?"

"I did."

He could hear Lindsey shuffling around in the background.

"You know come hell or high water, I will be there to support you and Chelsea. And I'll look sexy as hell in a suit, standing up there being the best man."

Ben rolled his eyes.

"But—but," he repeated. "The two of you better have your shit together. That's not a lot of time, brother."

Ben sighed. "I know. To be honest, I think the time apart, reflecting over everything that happened, did a lot of the work. Hindsight and all, you see where shit went wrong, and how you could have fixed it. How you should have fixed it, you know."

"I can understand that."

"And it's good, Linds. I don't think I've had a single day where I haven't been scared this is all some dream I'm going to wake up from."

Ben went on to tell his best friend how far they had come in working on fixing what happened in the past.

He took a deep breath. "And that leads me to something else. I saw Veronica today."

Lindsey was quiet for a long time.

"Now. I'm going to have to go get myself checked out at a doctor because I could have sworn I just heard you say that you saw Veronica. Today."

Another deep breath. "I did."

"Well, motherfucker, you lead with that! What is wrong with you?! What in the hell did she want? That don't even matter. What did Chelsea say? Is she okay? Are *you* okay?"

Ben rubbed a large hand down his face. "I didn't tell her yet."

"You don't get to call me all prepared to marry this girl—again—and talk about how far you two have come in working shit out and then drop that bomb on me. And—*and*—say you haven't even told her. No."

"We just got engaged days ago, Linds! She was at home with her best friends telling them the news and planning shit out. I went to the store to get some food to make, and I just wanted to go, get what I needed, come home and celebrate with her favorite people. And there was Veronica, in the fucking store. I almost ran her over by accident. And then again on fucking purpose."

"And you didn't tell Chelsea?"

"I didn't want to ruin it."

"And after everyone went home?" Lindsey pressed.

"I don't know. The last fucking thing I want to have to tell her is the woman who destroyed us the first time is suddenly just casually walking around shopping in Saltridge. And that I saw her, and I talked to her."

"And then you hid it from her."

Ben sighed. "I don't want to hurt her or scare her. I don't want to fight with her and lose her all over again. I can't, Linds."

"I understand that. I do. But this is what's going to make you lose her more. She's Chelsea. And *she's* Veronica, and you know the chances of her just poofing away aren't so great. Chelsea will find out one way or another, and I can tell you that cute little blonde firecracker of yours is going to be a lot more pissed off at you for not telling her than she ever would be at you breaking the news to her in the first place."

Ben made an annoyed sound into the phone.

"How about you fix this shit *and then* you can call me and ask me about being your best man."

Ben hung his head down a little and let what Lindsey was saying sink in.

"And in the meantime, maybe y'all should think about planning the wedding for next year. What's the problem in that? Three months. You have a lot of shit to get squared away. You're already together. What's the rush?"

"A baby."

Lindsey made some strangled noise.

"What the fuck do you mean, a baby!?"

Ben held the phone slightly back from his ear. "Relax, there's not a baby. Not yet anyway, at least I don't there is."

"Oh fuck you, Benjamin. You don't *think* there's a baby? What does that even mean? Wear a damn condom. Jesus Christ, listen to me. I'm going to hang up this phone, and you're going to go wake Chelsea up and tell her about Veronica. Then, you're going to super glue a damn condom to your dick for the next 90 days. You got it?"

Ben knew there was no use in attempting to dive into the whole baby issue with Lindsey. He wouldn't understand. The closest thing he had ever had to a long-term relationship was with him, and there definitely weren't any damn babies in their future.

Besides, Lindsey's head might explode if he threw anything else at him tonight. Agreeing to do as he said, Ben hung up the phone. He knew what he needed to do, but that didn't make this any easier.

Sometime later, Ben crept up the stairs. As he stood in the doorway watching Chelsea sleep, he said a quick prayer that what he was about to do wouldn't be the start of another war between them. His first instinct was to pretend the whole run in with Veronica never happened. But Lindsey was right, Veronica was bound to make another appearance. Especially now that they bumped into each other. If there was ever a woman he had it wrong about, it was Veronica. Now that he knew what her brother did to Chelsea, he wouldn't put anything past her. She was always strange, but now he questioned her sanity.

Stripping down to his boxers, Ben made his way to the bathroom. He brushed his teeth and washed his face. Truth was, he was stalling, and he knew it. Relenting to his fate, he crawled into bed and scooted up behind Chelsea. She was in one of his old shirts, which had again become one of her sleeping staples. He inched his hand underneath the fabric until he could spread his fingers across her flat stomach.

Welcoming the distraction, he allowed his thoughts to drift. He spent so much time deflecting conversations about their future lately, sometimes he almost forgot how much he wanted all the things, only she was brave enough to voice.

Brushing the hair back from her neck, he placed a soft kiss just below her ear.

"Baby, wake up."

Chelsea stirred, stretching her arms out. She yawned loudly before grumbling something that he couldn't make out which caused him to smile.

Brushing his lips against hers, he nipped and teased her back to consciousness.

"Ben?"

Placing an elbow on each side of her head, he knew trapping her in bed like this was wrong, but he was going to use any means necessary to ensure that she heard him out. He couldn't let her mind start traveling down those dark paths again.

"We need to talk."

"What's wrong?" she asked, wrapping her arms around him.

"I saw Veronica today."

As soon as the words left his mouth, he wanted to take them back. Time itself seemed to freeze as Chelsea's mossy eyes slowly blinked open.

He couldn't lose her, not again, not when they were so close to reaching their happily ever after.

Not because of fucking Veronica.

Chelsea looked confused.

Then she closed her eyes again.

"Where?"

Ben wiped away a tear that rolled down her cheek.

"Earlier today. At the grocery store." His head shook. "I swear, Chelsea, I turned around, and she was just there."

"Did you talk to her?"

"Just for a second. Basically I just asked her what in the hell she was doing here, and I told her that if she knew what was good for her, she would get the fuck out of town."

Ben was wearing a look that she hadn't seen since their divorce. He seemed devastated. As though he really expected her to walk away from him because he ran into Veronica. Hadn't she just promised him a couple days ago that she wasn't going anywhere?

Her heart broke for him. She was so lost in her own grief over what happened between them, she really hadn't taken the time to think about everything he had been through. She hated Veronica. She hated that she hated Veronica. More than anything she wished she could forget that the delusional woman existed. But it wasn't looking like that was going to happen now that she was hanging around the local supermarket.

Still, it was well past time to show Ben that she wasn't going anywhere and that things weren't going to happen the same way as before.

When Chelsea felt him trembling against her, she knew she must have taken too long to say or do something. She pulled him down to her.

Ben's head buried in the crook of her neck, and right away she could feel dampness forming from the tears he was shedding.

All because of his fear of losing her again.

He hugged her tightly as she rubbed one of her small hands up and down his back. The other tangled up in his dark locks. She was about to ask him if he had any idea why she was here but then he started acting almost like she had the other day, breaking out into endless rambling apologies and repeating that he only saw her for a moment.

Chelsea closed her eyes and pulled him tighter.

"Ben, I know," she whispered. "It's okay. Please, look at me."

He slowly lifted his head, and she kissed him quickly.

"I have no idea why that woman has dared to even come around here or have the nerve to even speak to you," she said. "But it doesn't matter. It doesn't change anything. I'm horrified and angry that she's lurking around town, but I am not upset with you. I know that it's the last thing you want."

"She was just there." His voice still sounded as though he was pleading for her to believe him.

Chelsea kissed him again, this time with more force behind it.

"I know. And it does not change anything. I don't care about anything she does, says or tries to pull."

"I didn't want to tell you."

She didn't have to guess why. Not only was it written all over his handsome face, it was making the air around them tense and haunting.

"I'm not going anywhere, Ben."

Chelsea woke up without a stitch of clothing on, aching in all of her favorite ways but she couldn't see the cause of that anywhere.

"Ben?" The bed was cold.

Chelsea grabbed another one of his shirts as she searched through the house for him. It didn't take long. He was in his old office, sipping from a familiar mug. "You know I hate sleeping without you."

His eyes were sunken. "Sorry. I didn't want to wake you."

Chelsea crawled into his lap. "I love you."

"I love you, too. Always have."

"Come take a shower with me?" She kissed his cheek. "Please? Then maybe we can go downstairs and figure out something to eat?"

Chelsea was grateful their time in the shower perked Ben up. He was waiting for the worst. It made her stomach hurt.

"Nate thinks we should get married in Vegas."

Ben shook his head. "Nate and Holly should get married in Vegas, not us."

"But we could even have an Elvis."

"I thought this was a dream wedding, not a nightmare?"

Chelsea cuddled closer to him. "We should pick a place, though. We could do it here?"

Ben winced. "I don't like weddings in houses."

"Maybe we could see about having it at the hotel again. Or, well, maybe in a smaller room and everything, but I kind of keep going back to it."

"They did have that little courtyard you liked with the birdhouse gazebo thing."

She had forgotten all about it. "We can go look and put it down as a 'maybe'? If we don't think of anywhere else."

"Works for me."

Chelsea's teeth bit into her lip. "I want a photographer, lots of photos and videos."

"I assumed."

She loved her wedding photos and wanted it all captured again this second time as well.

"What about after?"

"What do you mean?" Chelsea asked. "I thought we had that planned out." She pointed to her stomach, "Baby."

Ben laughed. "I meant with the guests."

"Oh. Well, they're not invited for that part. That would just be awkward. Hmm, I don't know. Maybe everyone can come back here for a while?"

Ben looked up. "We could have dinner? Just close friends and family."

"I'm okay with that. I don't want all the silly things again. It was perfect the first time but that's just too much to recreate. Speeches, dances, games and then renting out some big space for it all. I don't need any of that."

Warm fingers stroked her back. "Okay," Ben nodded.

Chelsea pretzeled herself around him once more. "Ready to tell me what's really wrong?"

Veronica-Fucking-Pratt. He couldn't get her vapid face out of his mind. Or her bastard brother's. The Crafts moved together. It was how their family worked. It was too coincidental. Mitchell was waiting for her that night.

And Veronica fucking knew.

His arms tightened around her. "It's nothing you need to worry about."

"No secrets, remember?"

Ben sighed. "I saw Veronica, Chels. I know you don't want to think about it. But she worries me. Her family is powerful. I still think you should file a police report about what her brother did."

"What good would that do?"

"We could get a restraining order against her, file charges."

Chelsea sighed. "We're about to get married. I don't want to spend these months being constantly reminded of that night. Which is exactly what will happen if we start some legal battle. I don't like her hanging around here, either. But we've only seen her once. Maybe she really was just passing through or visiting someone."

"In Saltridge?"

"Maybe." Chelsea shrugged.

Ben closed his eyes, letting his head fall back against the sofa. "Doubtful," he said over a heavy sigh. "That family is fucking cancerous. I don't want her in this state much less our goddamn grocery store."

"I know," Chelsea said. Her soft lips pressed against his neck. "But Mitch is dead, and we're together. What's the worst she can do?"

Veronica Craft watched as the small marker on her screen quit moving.

Bingo. An address.

She switched the view to satellite and zoomed in on the house.

Mitchell would have his revenge.

To Be Continued…

A word from the Author

Thank you for reading Forgotten Vows. Benjamin and Chelsea's story has been a labor of love and resulted in countless sleepless nights. If you enjoyed this book, please consider leaving a review on Amazon. Reviews are the best way to support your favorite authors.

About the Author

Gayla J. Reel is a lover of all things angsty. Her husband is not a Rockstar. She is not a Vampire Slayer, and her children do not have superpowers. Gayla has never won the Nobel Peace Prize, nor does she plan to sell more books than The Bible. When she is not writing, Gayla is probably crying real tears because people won't stop talking to her.

Instagram: @authorgaylareel
TikTok: @authorgaylareel
Facebook: www.facebook.com/authorgaylareel
Email: gaylajreel@gmail.com

Made in the USA
Monee, IL
28 August 2025

23813555R00121